FIRE STARTERS

STORY BY JEN STORM
ILLUSTRATIONS BY SCOTT B. HENDERSON
COLOURS BY DONOVAN YACIUK

HIGHWATER
PRESS

For River James Storm. You are my world and everything I do I do for you. You gave me gifts of patience, growth, laughter, sweetness, all with a love I never fathomed possible. You're the reason I fight for the future now, and I want you to know how much you influence and amaze me every single day.

— J.S.

For Caleb and Bentleigh.

— S.B.H.

For Madelyn and Michelle.

— D.Y.

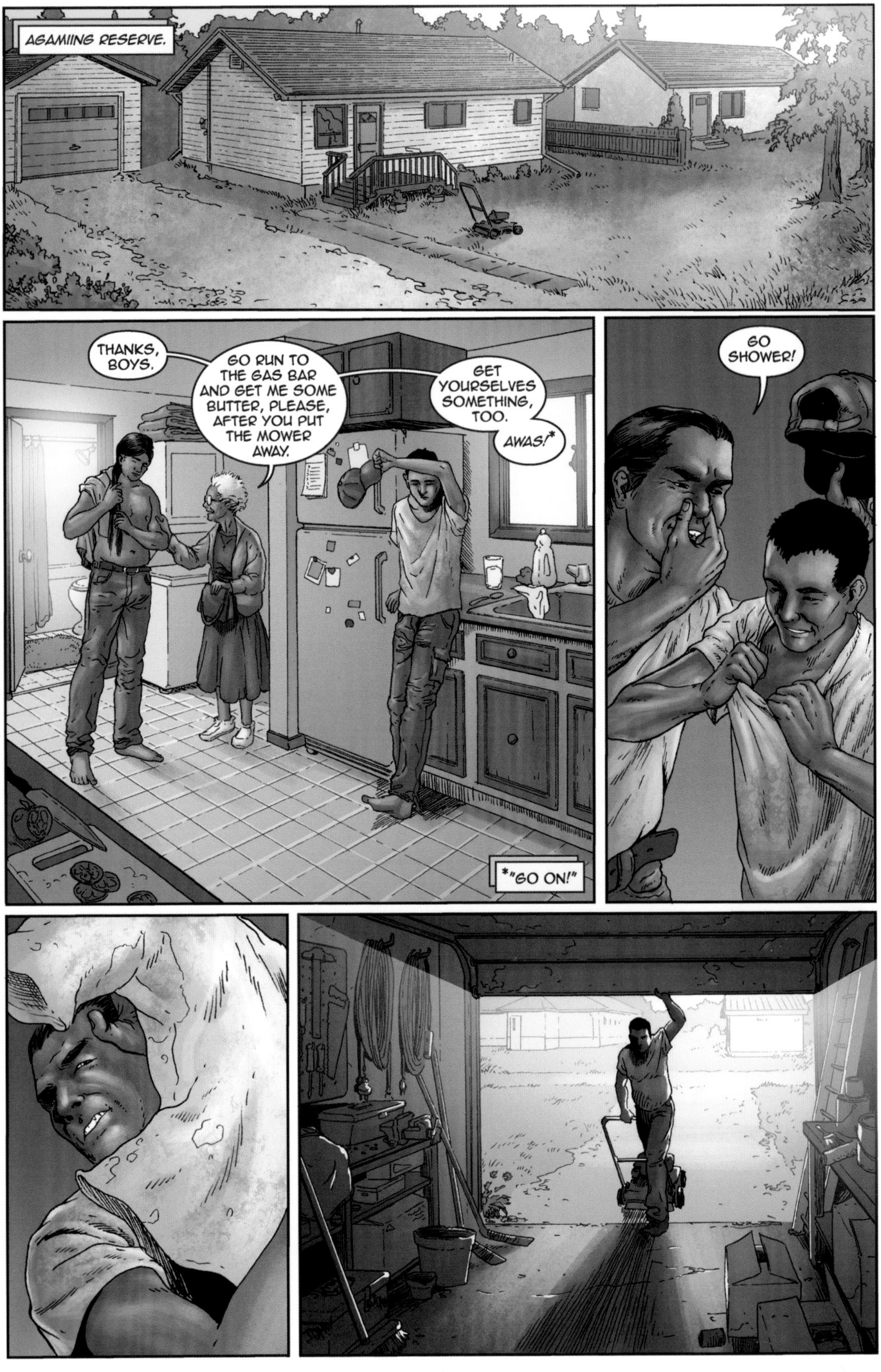
AGAMIING RESERVE.
THANKS, BOYS.
GO RUN TO THE GAS BAR AND GET ME SOME BUTTER, PLEASE, AFTER YOU PUT THE MOWER AWAY.
GET YOURSELVES SOMETHING, TOO.
AWAS!*
*"GO ON!"
GO SHOWER!

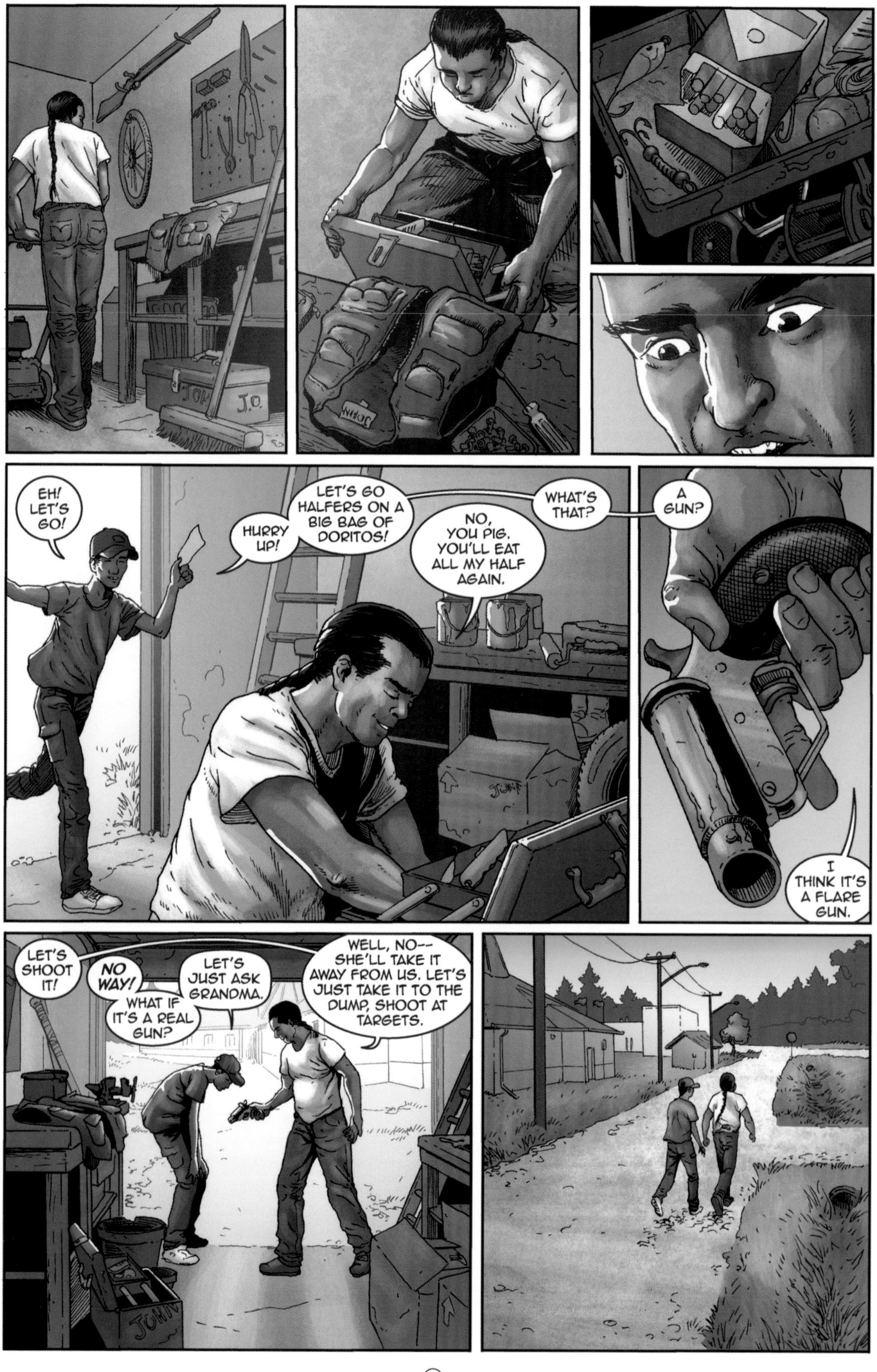

EH! LET'S GO!
HURRY UP!
LET'S GO HALFERS ON A BIG BAG OF DORITOS!
NO, YOU PIG. YOU'LL EAT ALL MY HALF AGAIN.
WHAT'S THAT?
A GUN?
I THINK IT'S A FLARE GUN.
LET'S SHOOT IT!
NO WAY! WHAT IF IT'S A REAL GUN?
LET'S JUST ASK GRANDMA.
WELL, NO-- SHE'LL TAKE IT AWAY FROM US. LET'S JUST TAKE IT TO THE DUMP, SHOOT AT TARGETS.

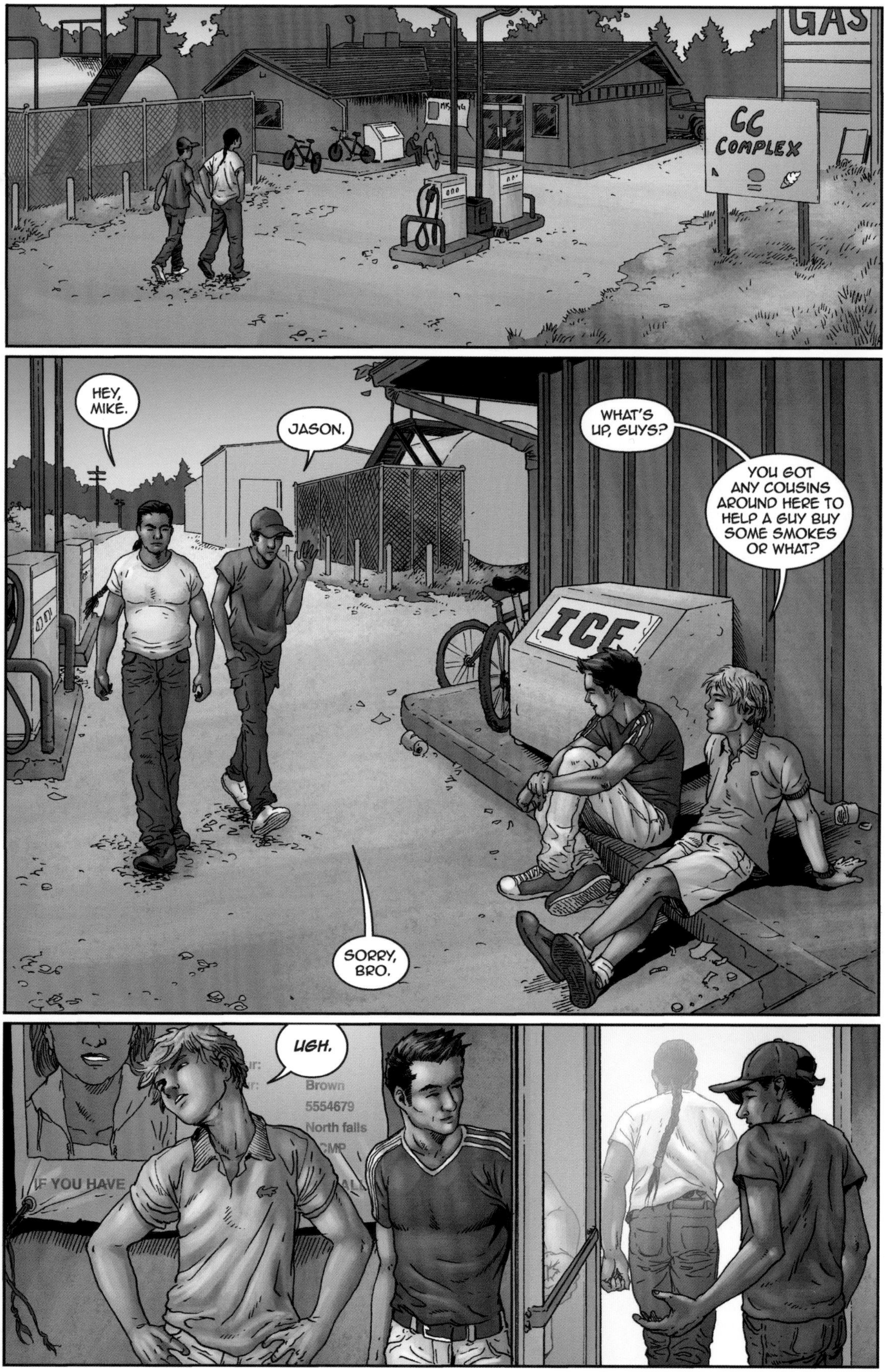
GAS
CC COMPLEX
HEY, MIKE.
JASON.
WHAT'S UP, GUYS?
YOU GOT ANY COUSINS AROUND HERE TO HELP A GUY BUY SOME SMOKES OR WHAT?
ICE
SORRY, BRO.
UGH.
Brown
5554679
North falls
IF YOU HAVE

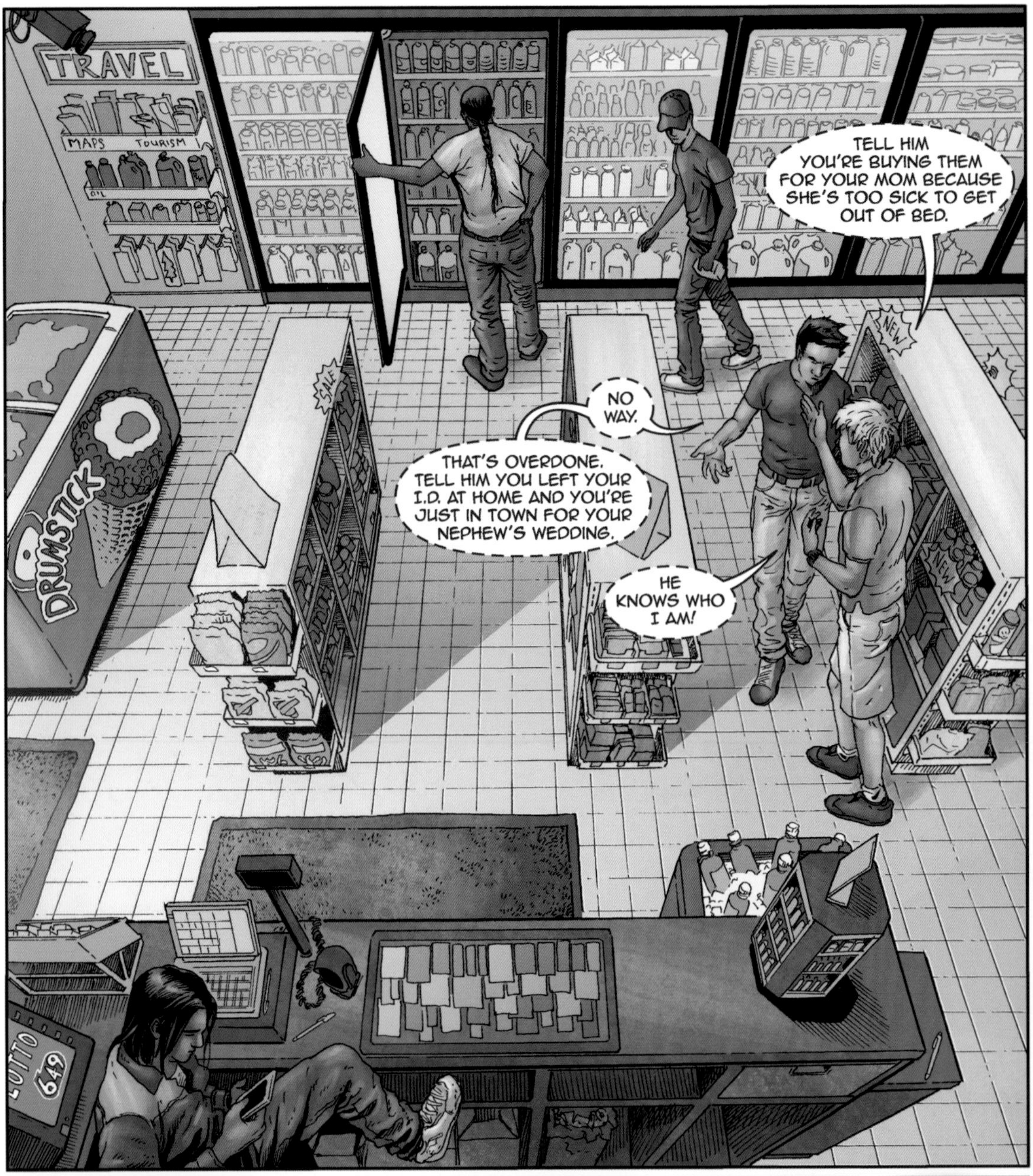
TRAVEL
MAPS
TOURISM
TELL HIM YOU'RE BUYING THEM FOR YOUR MOM BECAUSE SHE'S TOO SICK TO GET OUT OF BED.
NO WAY.
THAT'S OVERDONE. TELL HIM YOU LEFT YOUR I.D. AT HOME AND YOU'RE JUST IN TOWN FOR YOUR NEPHEW'S WEDDING.
HE KNOWS WHO I AM!
DRUMSTICK
SALE
NEW
LOTTO 649

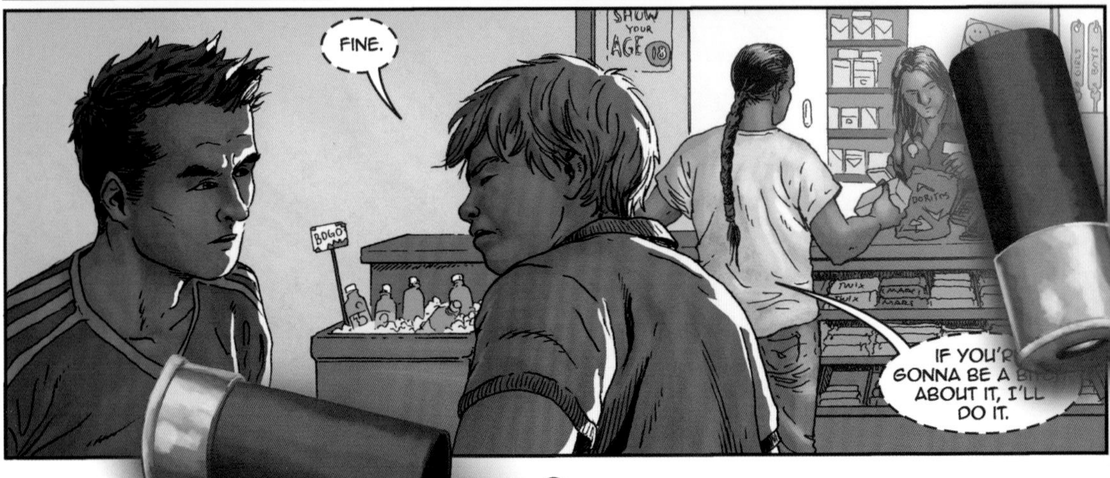
SHOW YOUR AGE 18
FINE.
BOGO
IF YOU'R
GONNA BE A B
ABOUT IT, I'LL
DO IT.

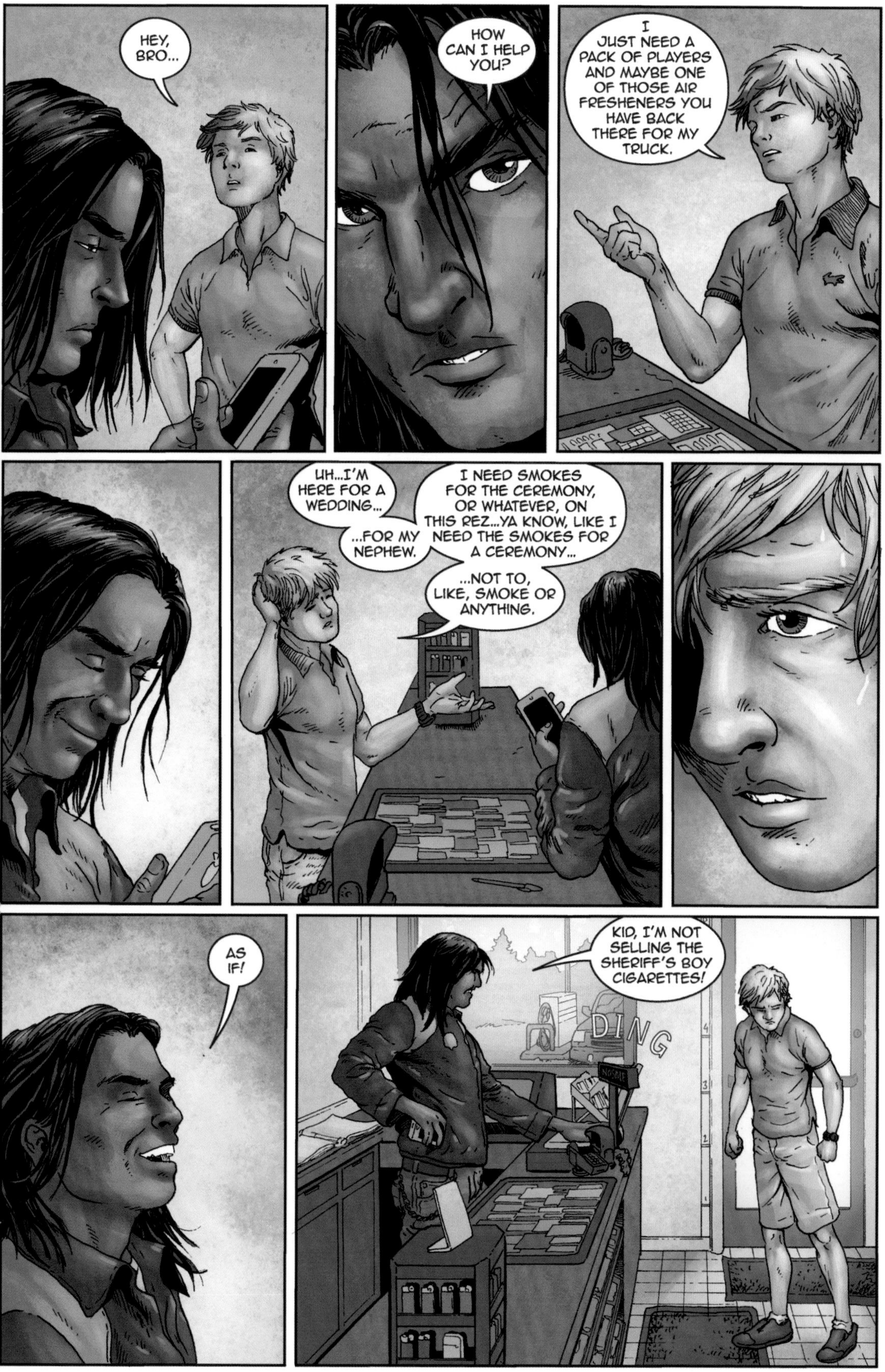
HEY, BRO...
HOW CAN I HELP YOU?
I JUST NEED A PACK OF PLAYERS AND MAYBE ONE OF THOSE AIR FRESHENERS YOU HAVE BACK THERE FOR MY TRUCK.
UH...I'M HERE FOR A WEDDING...
...FOR MY NEPHEW.
I NEED SMOKES FOR THE CEREMONY, OR WHATEVER, ON THIS REZ...YA KNOW, LIKE I NEED THE SMOKES FOR A CEREMONY...
...NOT TO, LIKE, SMOKE OR ANYTHING.
AS IF!
KID, I'M NOT SELLING THE SHERIFF'S BOY CIGARETTES!
DING

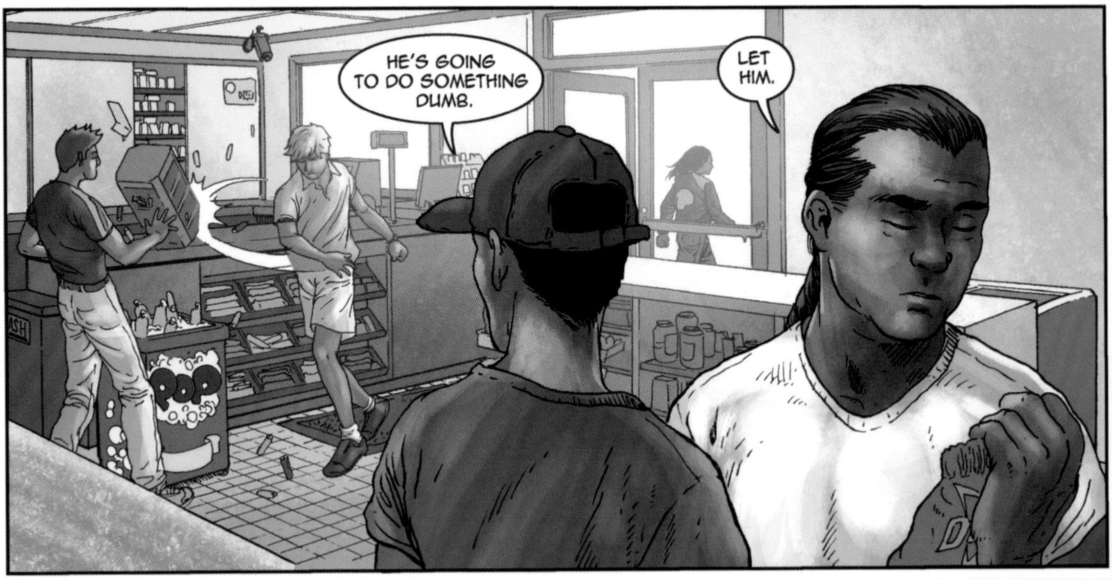
HE'S GOING TO DO SOMETHING DUMB.
LET HIM.

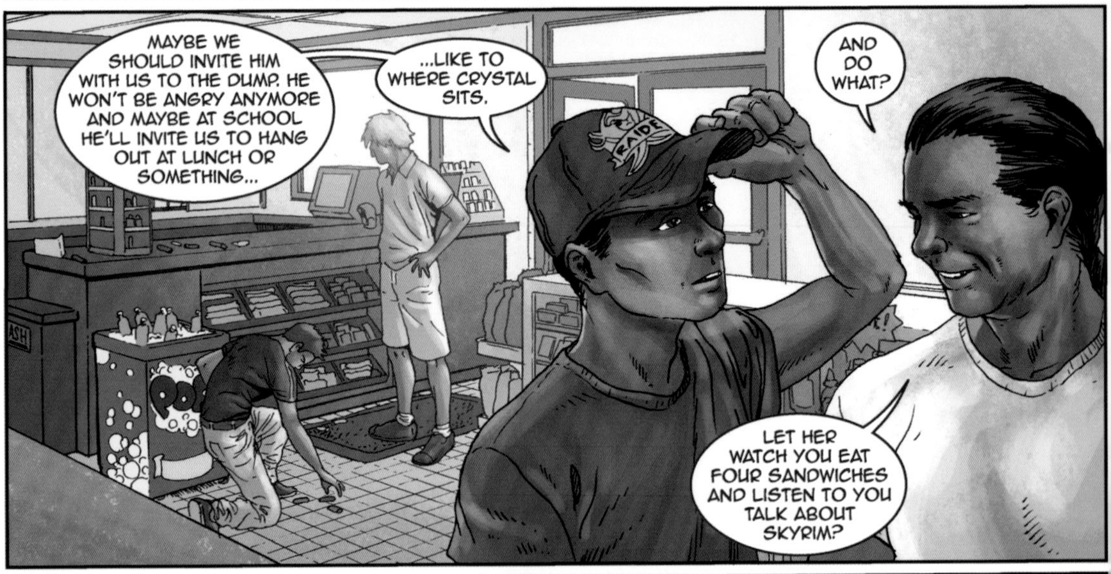
MAYBE WE SHOULD INVITE HIM WITH US TO THE DUMP. HE WON'T BE ANGRY ANYMORE AND MAYBE AT SCHOOL HE'LL INVITE US TO HANG OUT AT LUNCH OR SOMETHING...
...LIKE TO WHERE CRYSTAL SITS.
AND DO WHAT?
LET HER WATCH YOU EAT FOUR SANDWICHES AND LISTEN TO YOU TALK ABOUT SKYRIM?

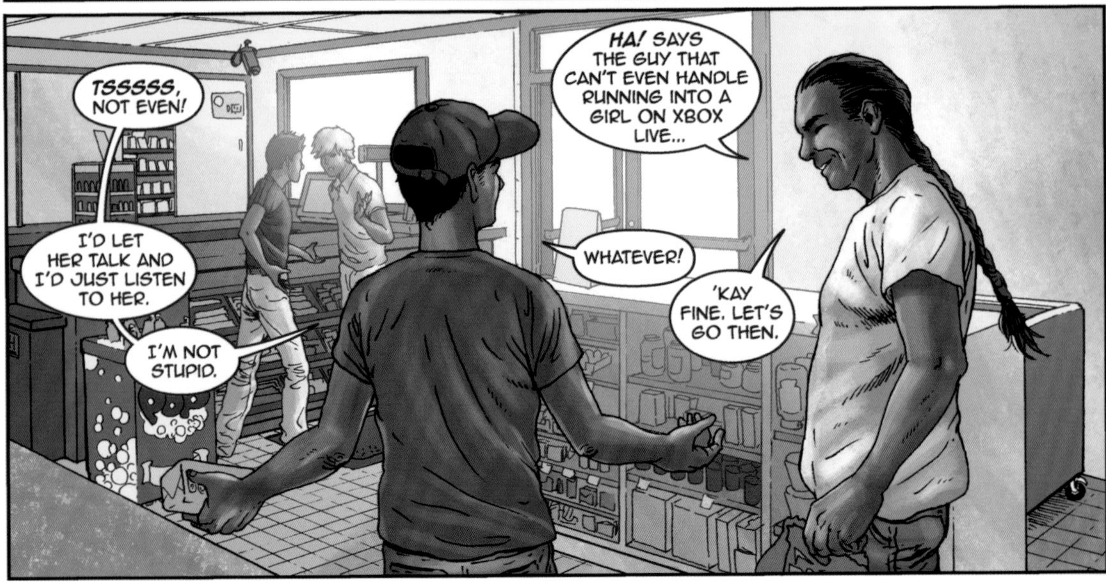
TSSSSS, NOT EVEN!
I'D LET HER TALK AND I'D JUST LISTEN TO HER.
I'M NOT STUPID.
HA! SAYS THE GUY THAT CAN'T EVEN HANDLE RUNNING INTO A GIRL ON XBOX LIVE...
WHATEVER!
'KAY FINE. LET'S GO THEN.

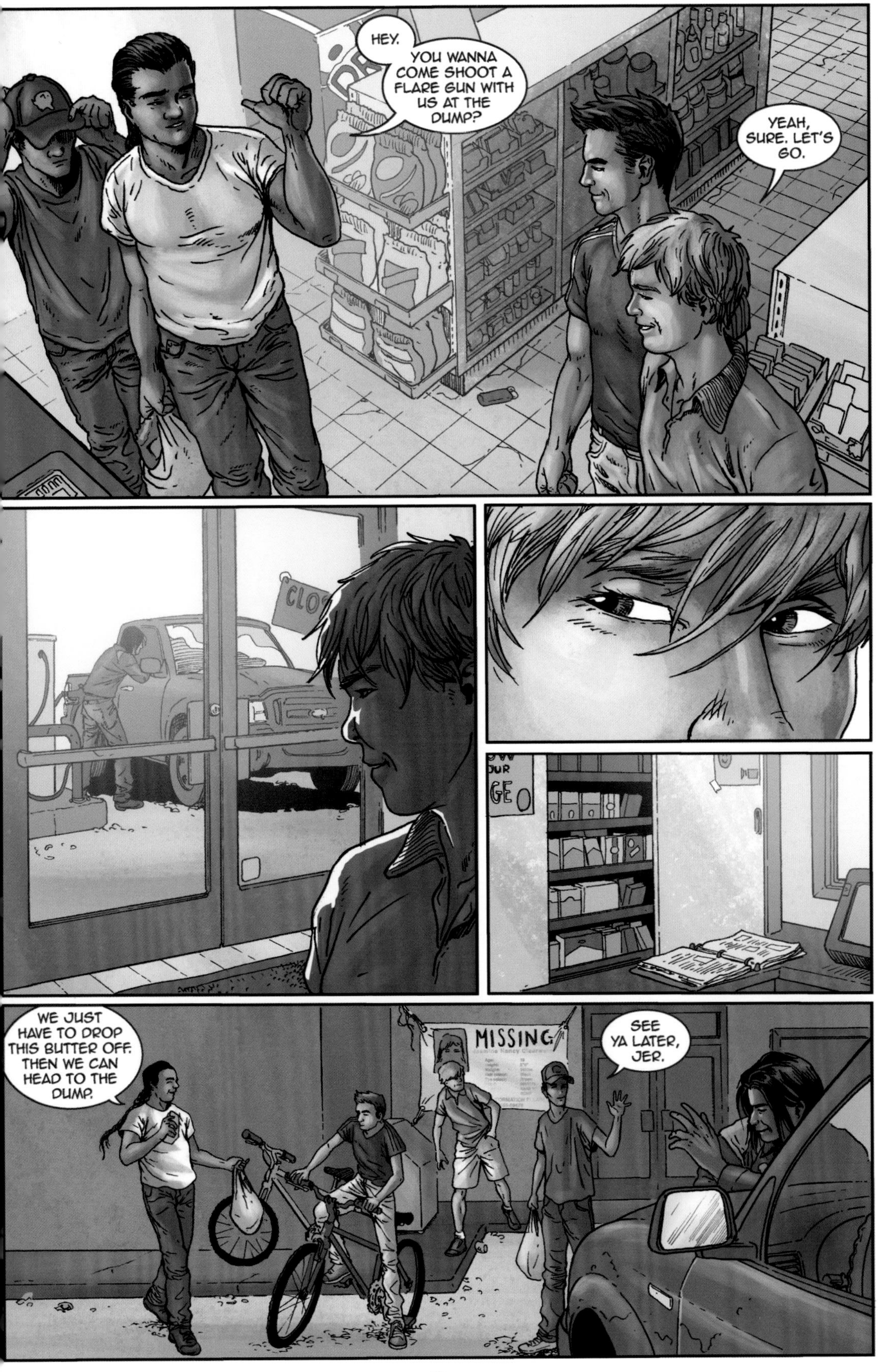
HEY.
YOU WANNA COME SHOOT A FLARE GUN WITH US AT THE DUMP?
YEAH, SURE. LET'S GO.
WE JUST HAVE TO DROP THIS BUTTER OFF. THEN WE CAN HEAD TO THE DUMP.
MISSING
SEE YA LATER, JER.

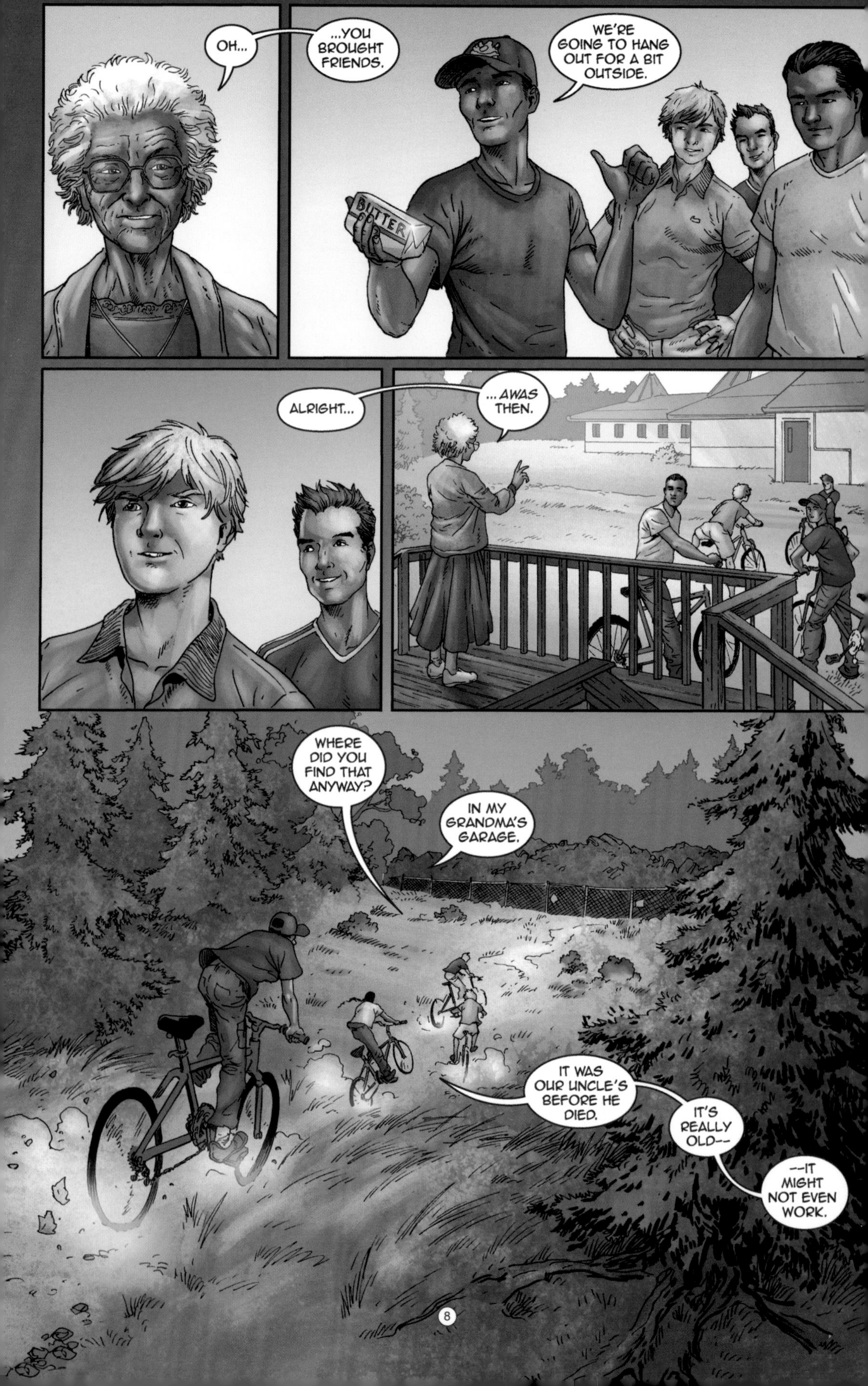
OH...
...YOU BROUGHT FRIENDS.
WE'RE GOING TO HANG OUT FOR A BIT OUTSIDE.
BUTTER
ALRIGHT...
...AWAS THEN.
WHERE DID YOU FIND THAT ANYWAY?
IN MY GRANDMA'S GARAGE.
IT WAS OUR UNCLE'S BEFORE HE DIED.
IT'S REALLY OLD--
--IT MIGHT NOT EVEN WORK.

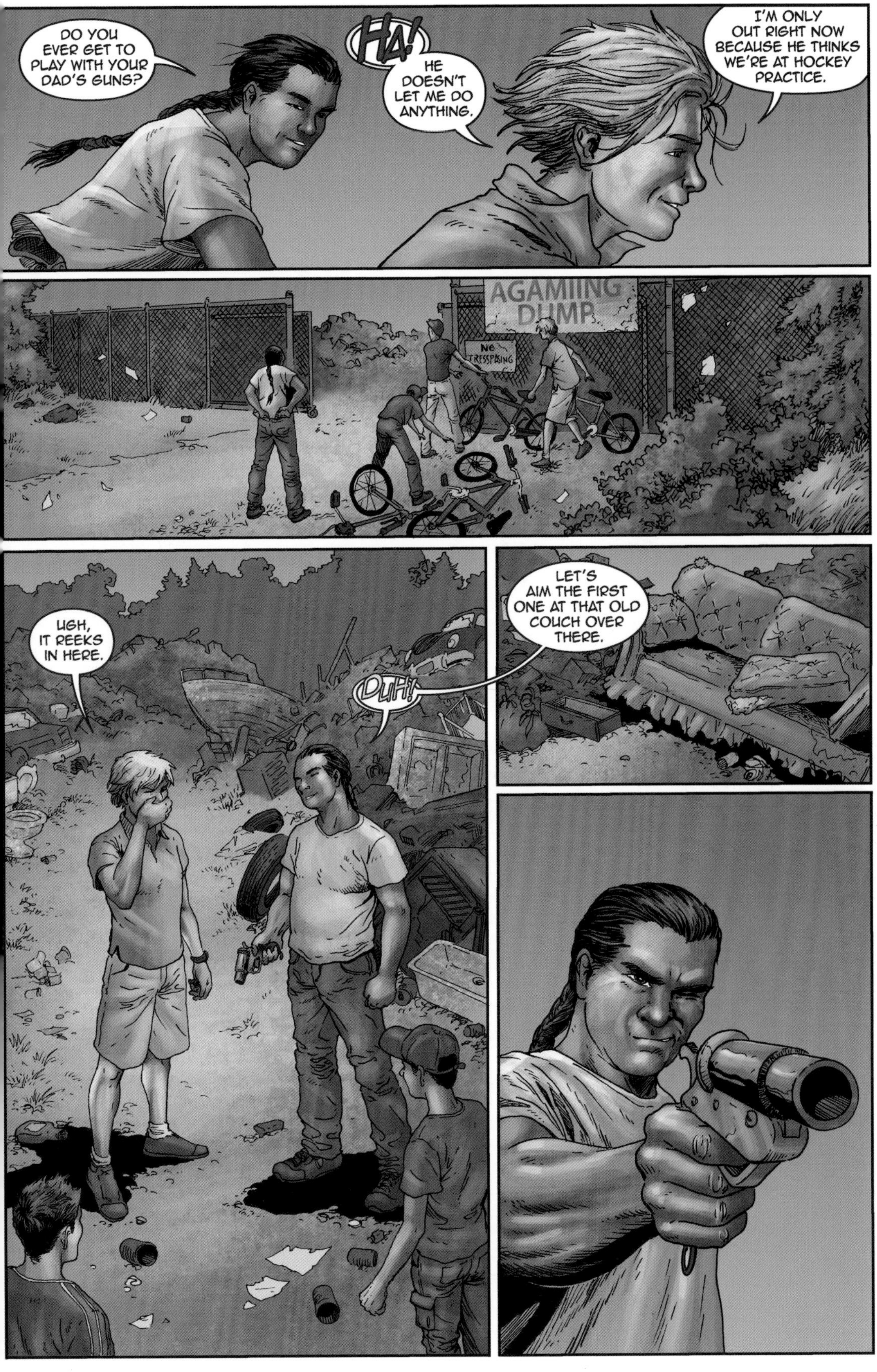

DO YOU EVER GET TO PLAY WITH YOUR DAD'S GUNS?
HA!
HE DOESN'T LET ME DO ANYTHING.
I'M ONLY OUT RIGHT NOW BECAUSE HE THINKS WE'RE AT HOCKEY PRACTICE.
AGAMIING DUMP
NO TRESPASING
UGH, IT REEKS IN HERE.
DUH!
LET'S AIM THE FIRST ONE AT THAT OLD COUCH OVER THERE.

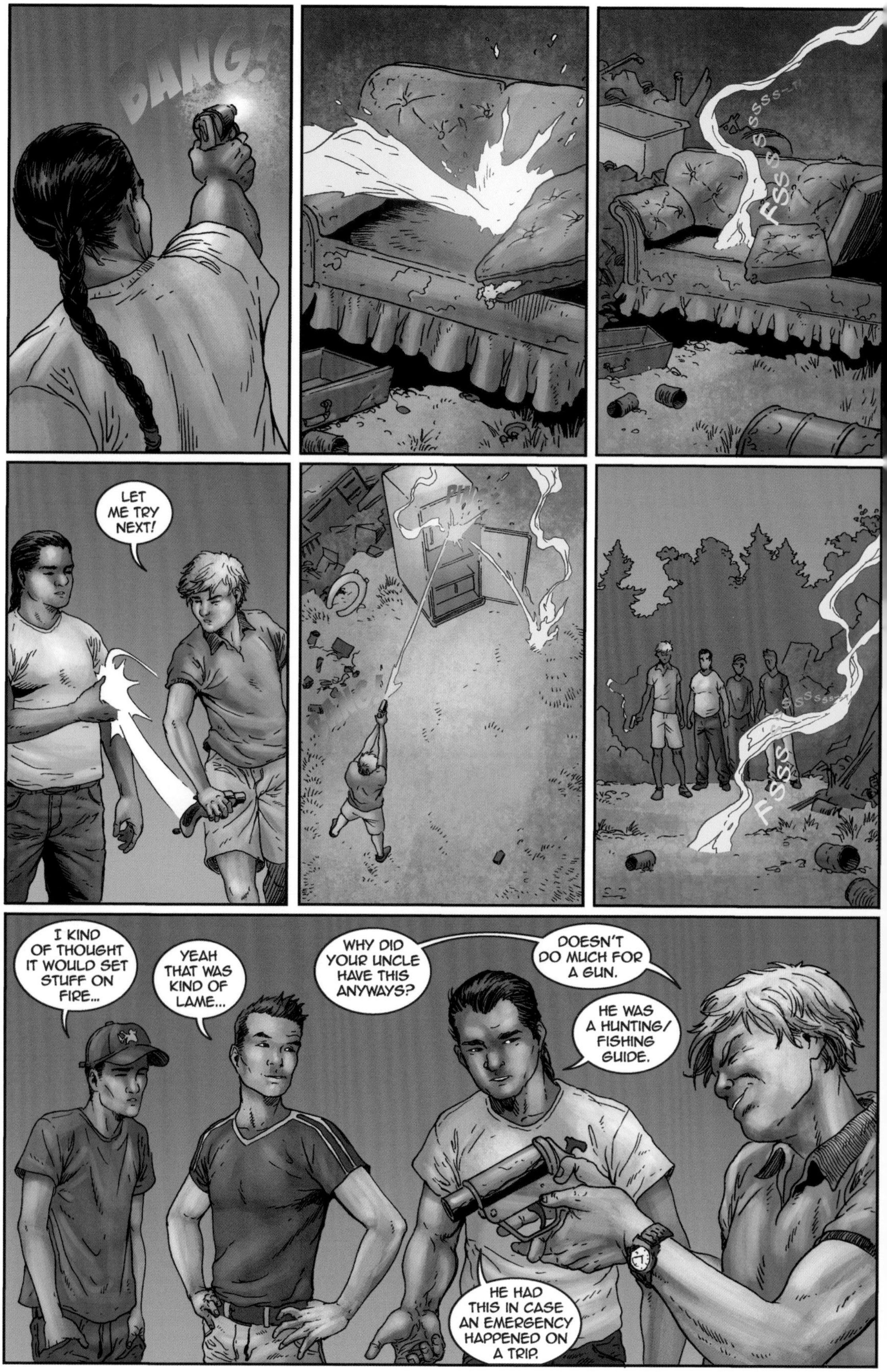
BANG!
FSSSSSSSSSsss-t!
LET ME TRY NEXT!
FSSSSSSSSsss-t!
I KIND OF THOUGHT IT WOULD SET STUFF ON FIRE...
YEAH THAT WAS KIND OF LAME...
WHY DID YOUR UNCLE HAVE THIS ANYWAYS?
DOESN'T DO MUCH FOR A GUN.
HE WAS A HUNTING/ FISHING GUIDE.
HE HAD THIS IN CASE AN EMERGENCY HAPPENED ON A TRIP.

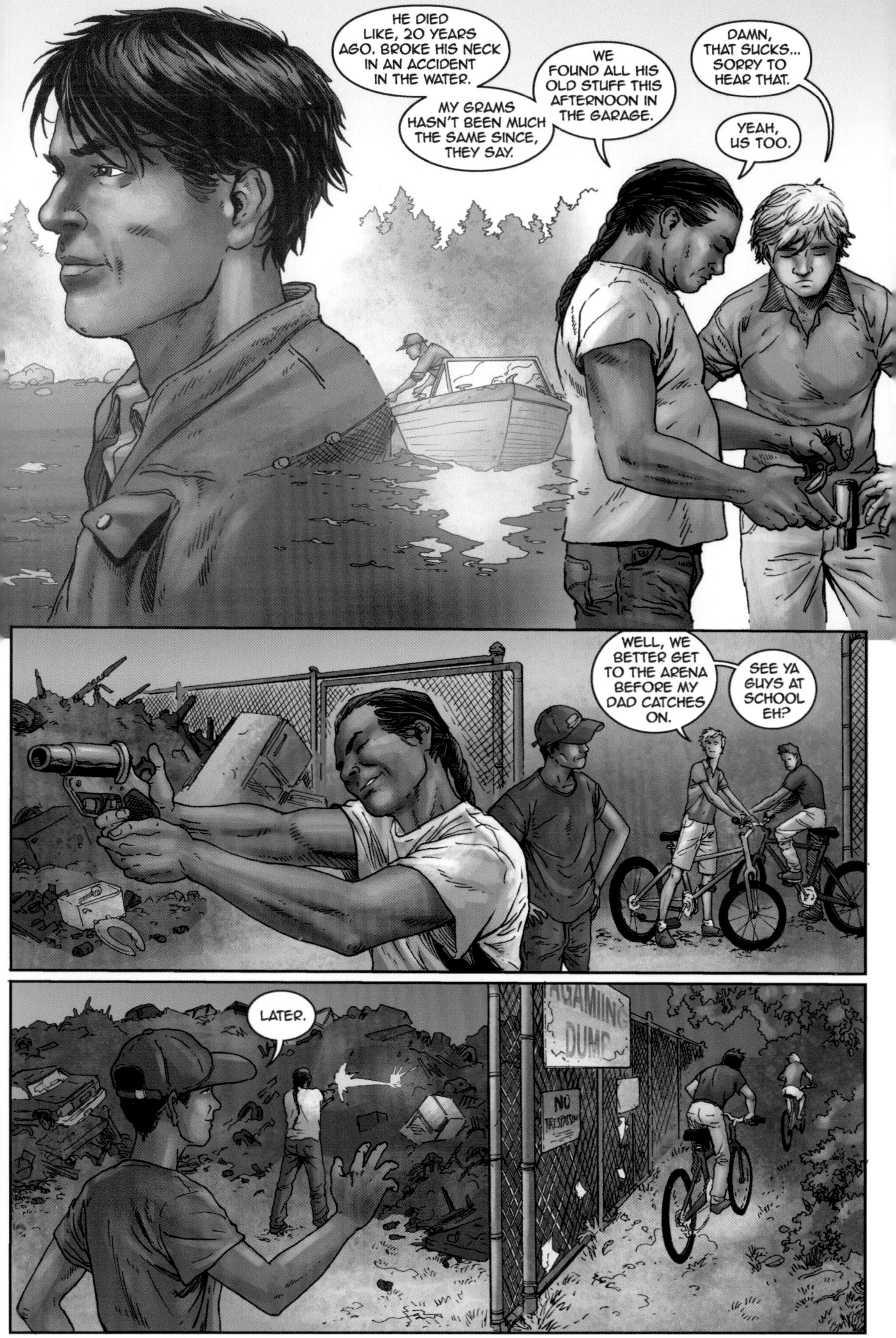
HE DIED LIKE, 20 YEARS AGO. BROKE HIS NECK IN AN ACCIDENT IN THE WATER.
MY GRAMS HASN'T BEEN MUCH THE SAME SINCE, THEY SAY.
WE FOUND ALL HIS OLD STUFF THIS AFTERNOON IN THE GARAGE.
DAMN, THAT SUCKS... SORRY TO HEAR THAT.
YEAH, US TOO.
WELL, WE BETTER GET TO THE ARENA BEFORE MY DAD CATCHES ON.
SEE YA GUYS AT SCHOOL EH?
LATER.

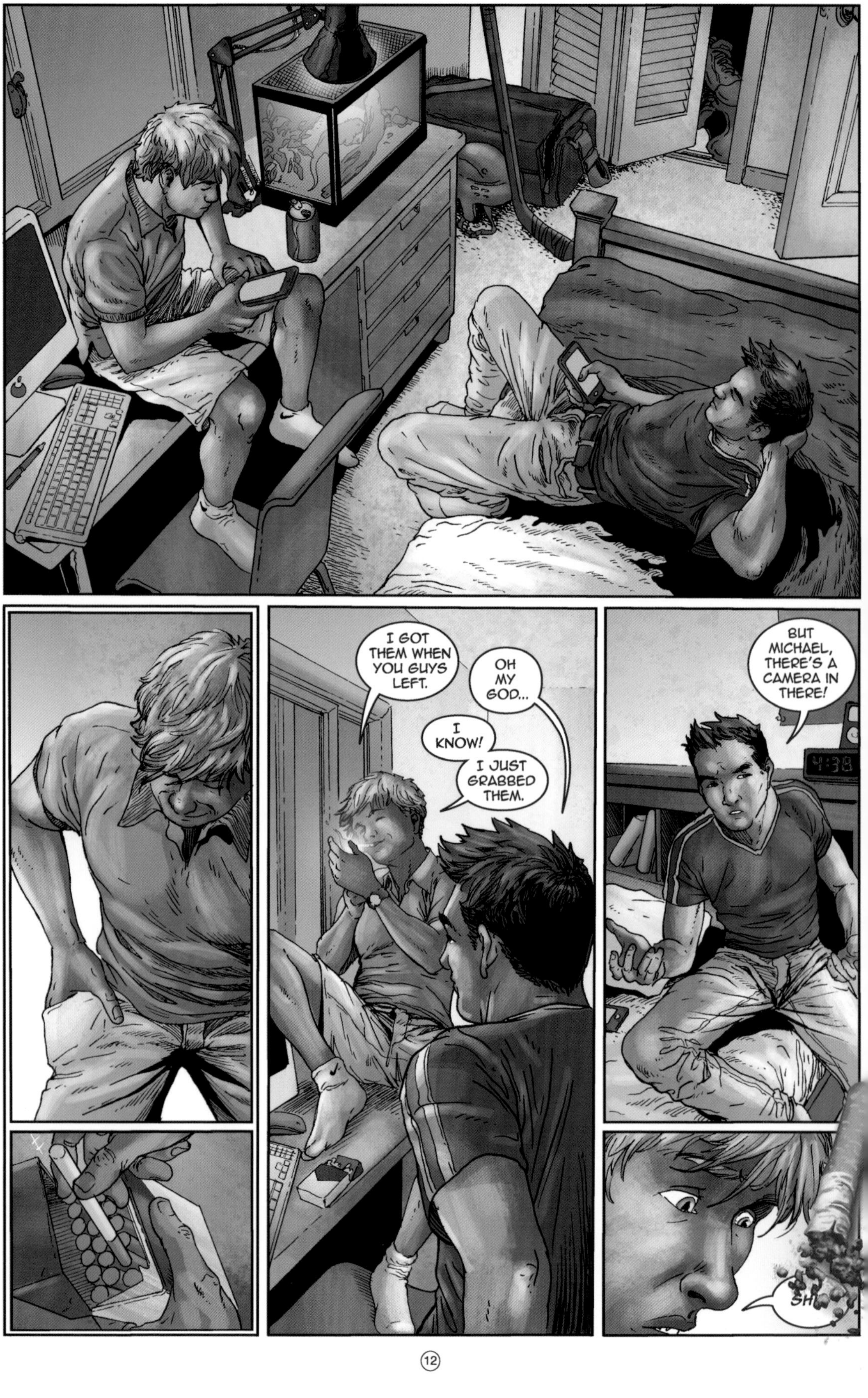
I GOT THEM WHEN YOU GUYS LEFT.
OH MY GOD...
I KNOW!
I JUST GRABBED THEM.
BUT MICHAEL, THERE'S A CAMERA IN THERE!
SH

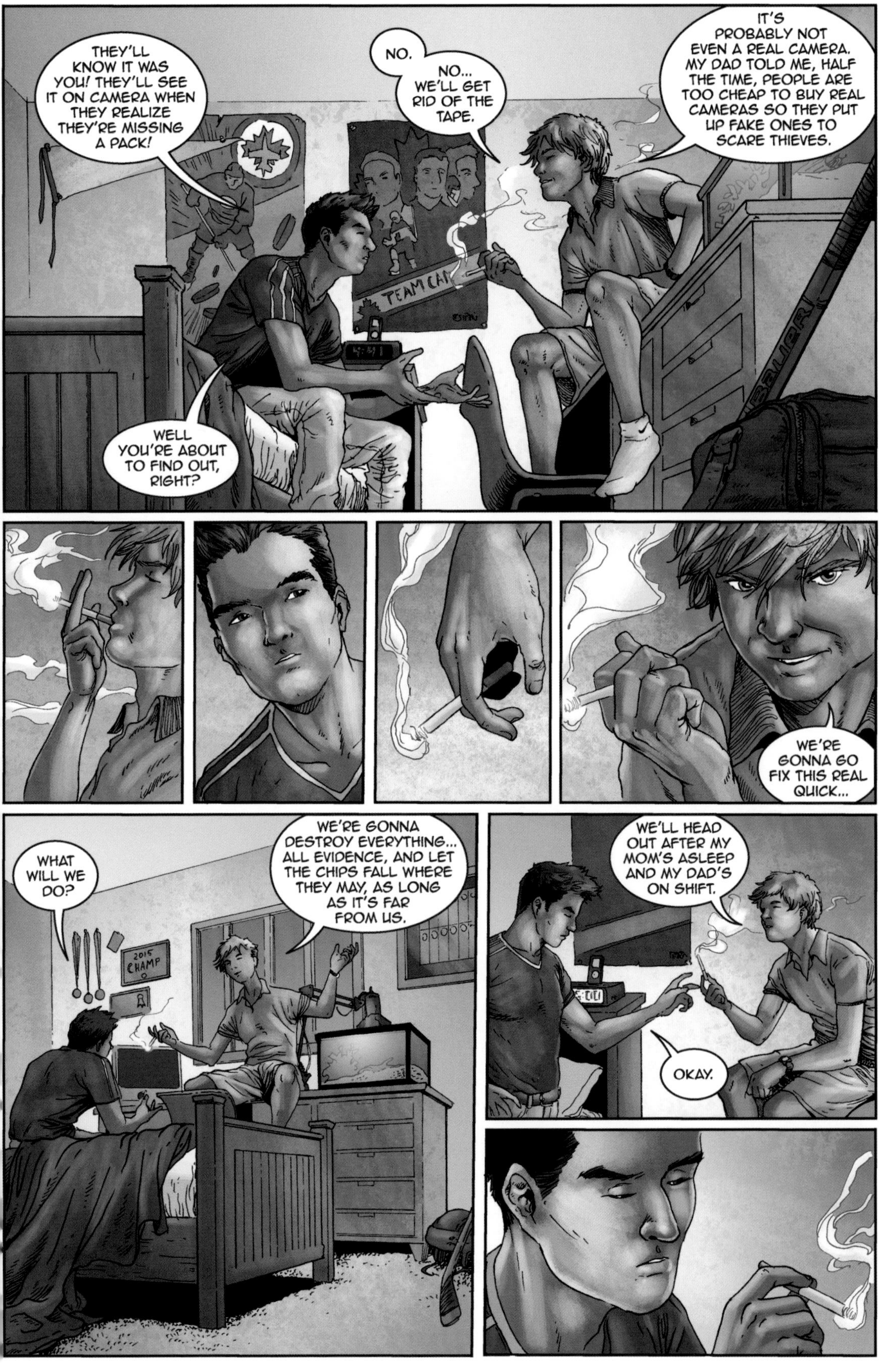
THEY'LL KNOW IT WAS YOU! THEY'LL SEE IT ON CAMERA WHEN THEY REALIZE THEY'RE MISSING A PACK!
NO.
NO... WE'LL GET RID OF THE TAPE.
IT'S PROBABLY NOT EVEN A REAL CAMERA. MY DAD TOLD ME, HALF THE TIME, PEOPLE ARE TOO CHEAP TO BUY REAL CAMERAS SO THEY PUT UP FAKE ONES TO SCARE THIEVES.
WELL YOU'RE ABOUT TO FIND OUT, RIGHT?
TEAM CA
WE'RE GONNA GO FIX THIS REAL QUICK...
WHAT WILL WE DO?
WE'RE GONNA DESTROY EVERYTHING... ALL EVIDENCE, AND LET THE CHIPS FALL WHERE THEY MAY, AS LONG AS IT'S FAR FROM US.
2015 CHAMP
WE'LL HEAD OUT AFTER MY MOM'S ASLEEP AND MY DAD'S ON SHIFT.
OKAY.

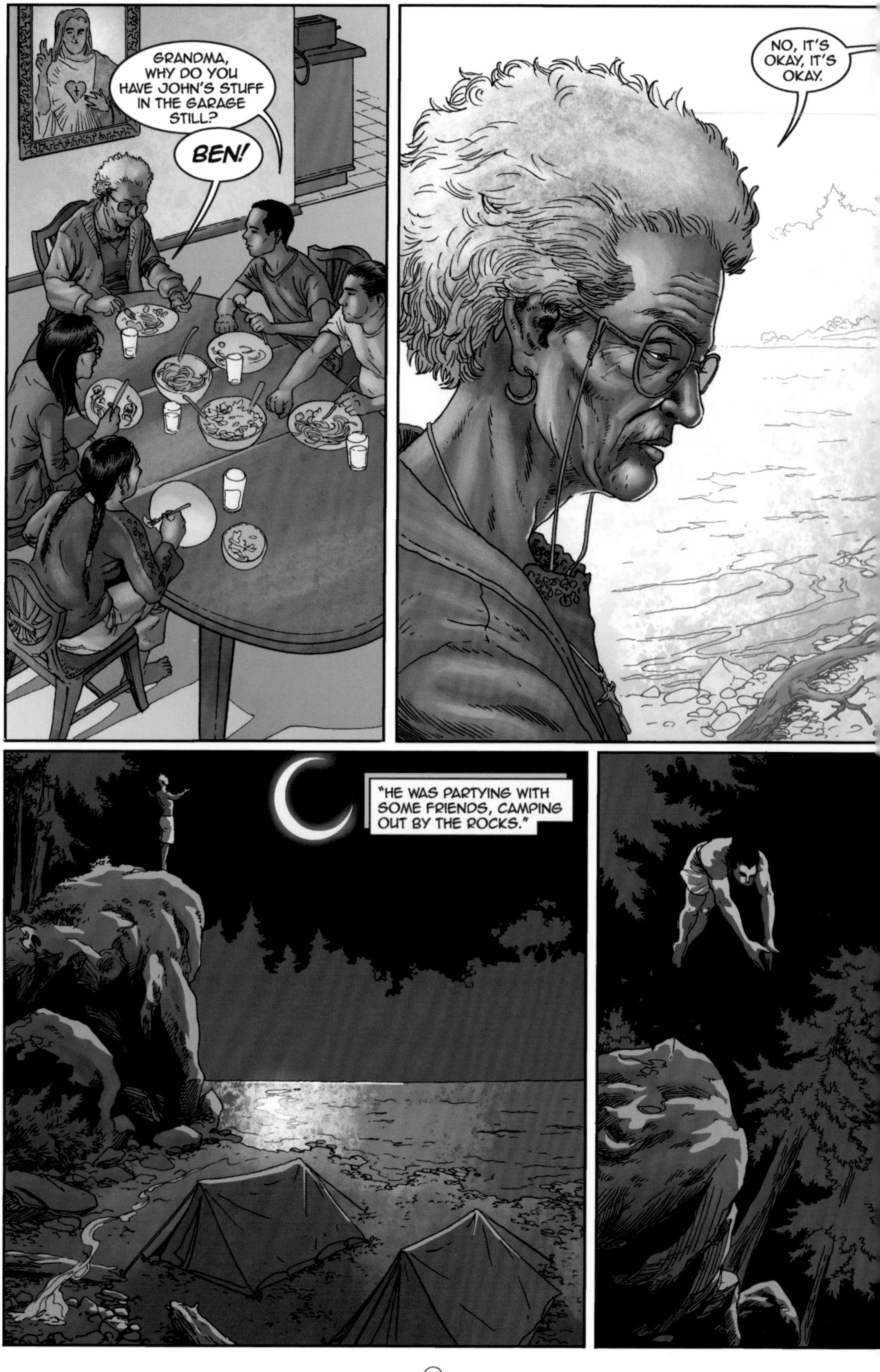

GRANDMA, WHY DO YOU HAVE JOHN'S STUFF IN THE GARAGE STILL?
BEN!
NO, IT'S OKAY, IT'S OKAY.
"HE WAS PARTYING WITH SOME FRIENDS, CAMPING OUT BY THE ROCKS."

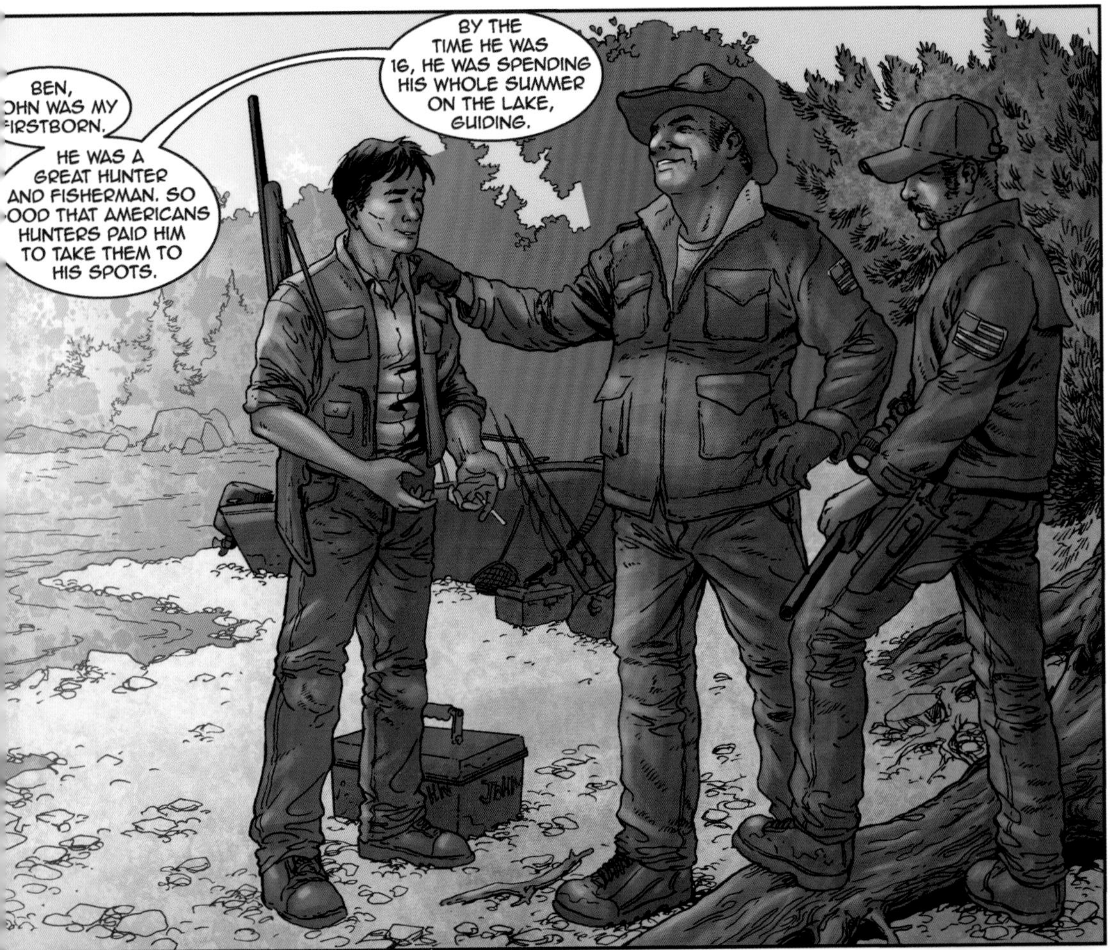
BEN, JOHN WAS MY FIRSTBORN.
HE WAS A GREAT HUNTER AND FISHERMAN. SO GOOD THAT AMERICANS HUNTERS PAID HIM TO TAKE THEM TO HIS SPOTS.
BY THE TIME HE WAS 16, HE WAS SPENDING HIS WHOLE SUMMER ON THE LAKE, GUIDING.

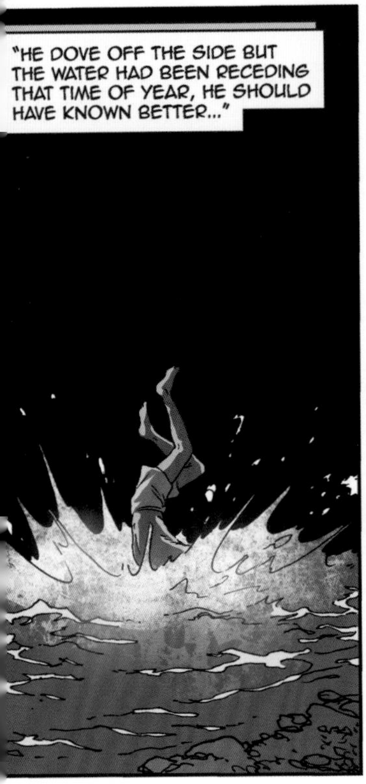
"HE DOVE OFF THE SIDE BUT THE WATER HAD BEEN RECEDING THAT TIME OF YEAR, HE SHOULD HAVE KNOWN BETTER..."

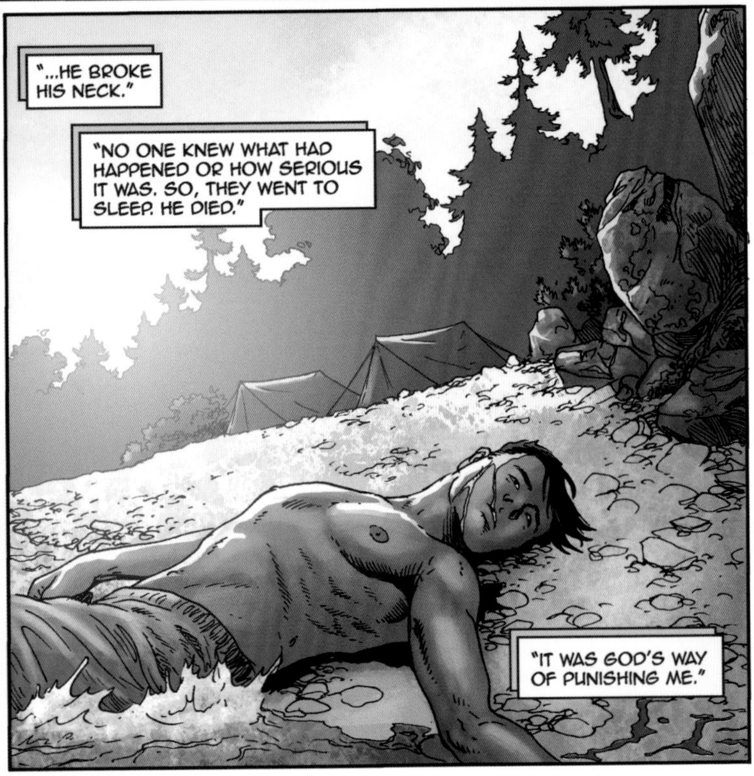
"...HE BROKE HIS NECK."
"NO ONE KNEW WHAT HAD HAPPENED OR HOW SERIOUS IT WAS. SO, THEY WENT TO SLEEP. HE DIED."
"IT WAS GOD'S WAY OF PUNISHING ME."

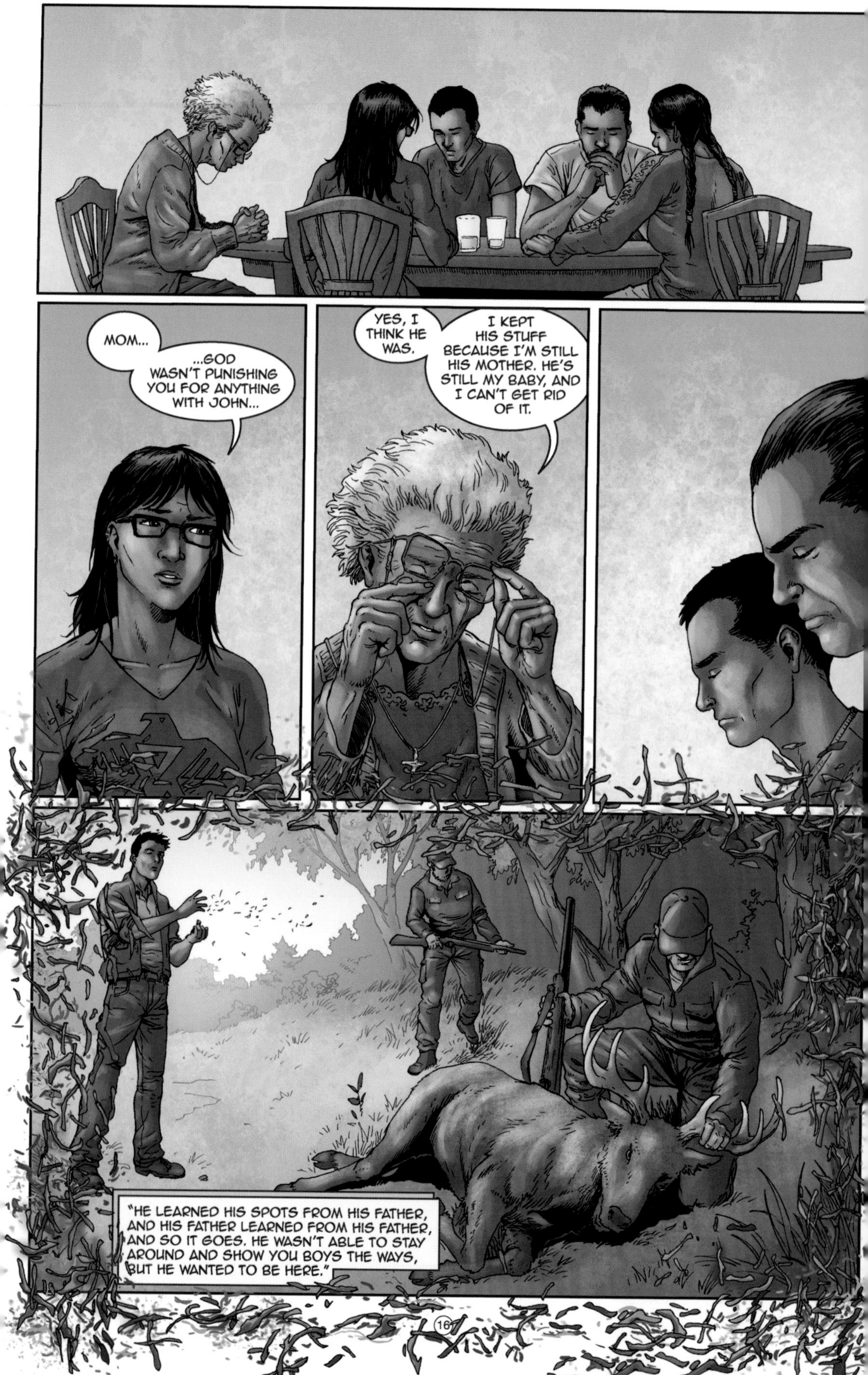
MOM...
...GOD WASN'T PUNISHING YOU FOR ANYTHING WITH JOHN...
YES, I THINK HE WAS.
I KEPT HIS STUFF BECAUSE I'M STILL HIS MOTHER. HE'S STILL MY BABY, AND I CAN'T GET RID OF IT.
"HE LEARNED HIS SPOTS FROM HIS FATHER, AND HIS FATHER LEARNED FROM HIS FATHER, AND SO IT GOES. HE WASN'T ABLE TO STAY AROUND AND SHOW YOU BOYS THE WAYS, BUT HE WANTED TO BE HERE."

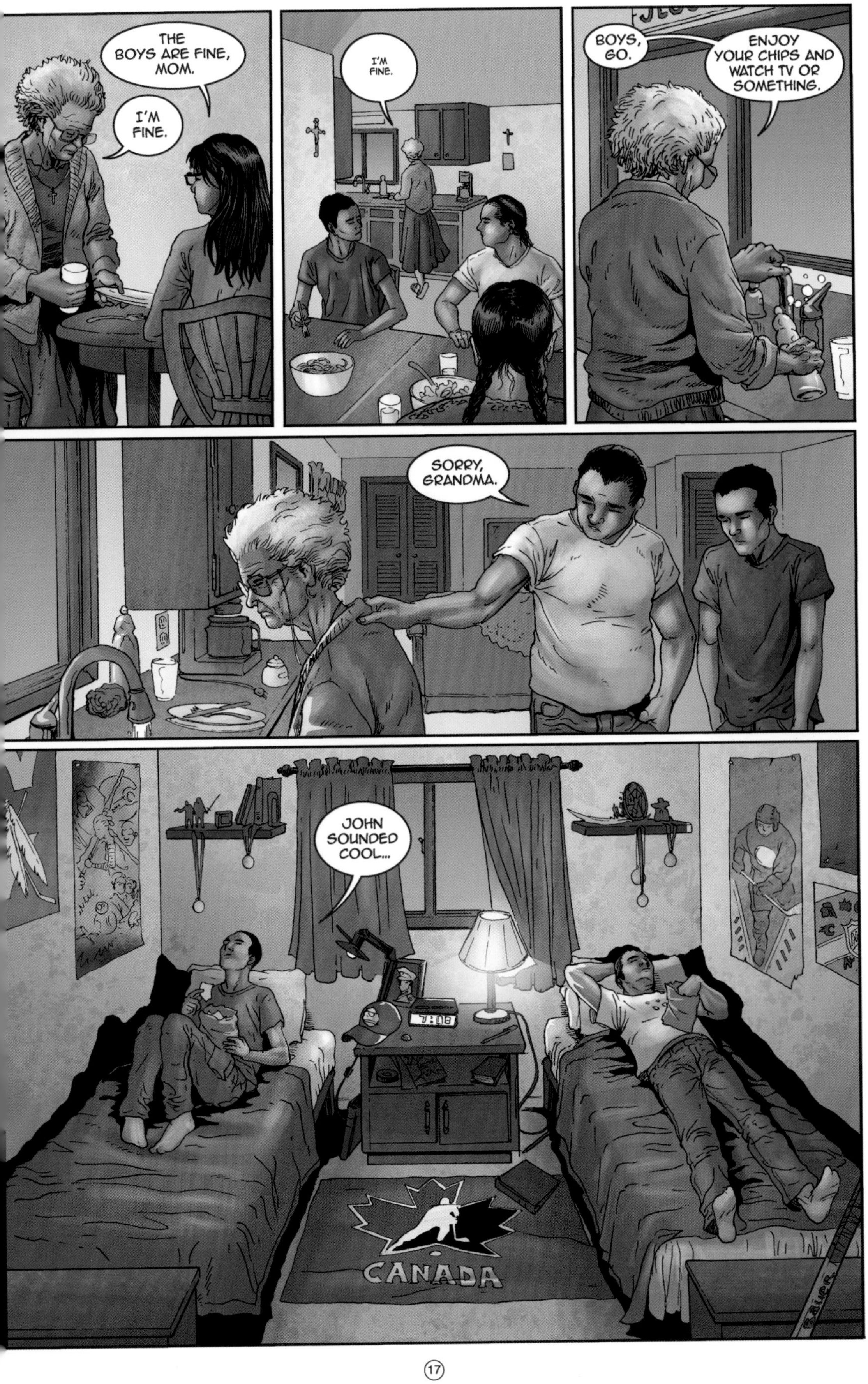
THE BOYS ARE FINE, MOM.
I'M FINE.
I'M FINE.
BOYS, GO.
ENJOY YOUR CHIPS AND WATCH TV OR SOMETHING.
SORRY, GRANDMA.
JOHN SOUNDED COOL...
CANADA

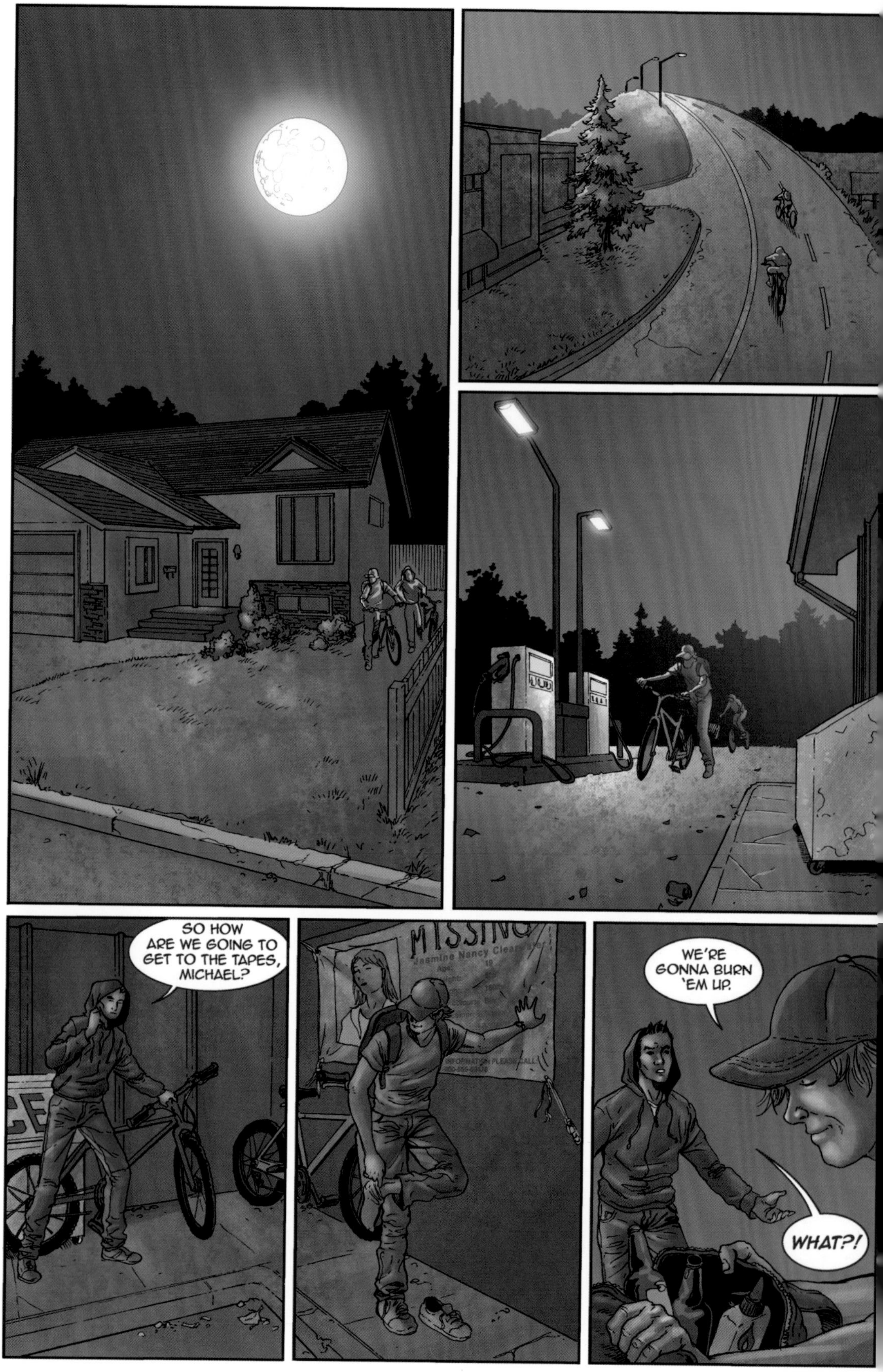

SO HOW ARE WE GOING TO GET TO THE TAPES, MICHAEL?
MISSING
WE'RE GONNA BURN 'EM UP.
WHAT?!

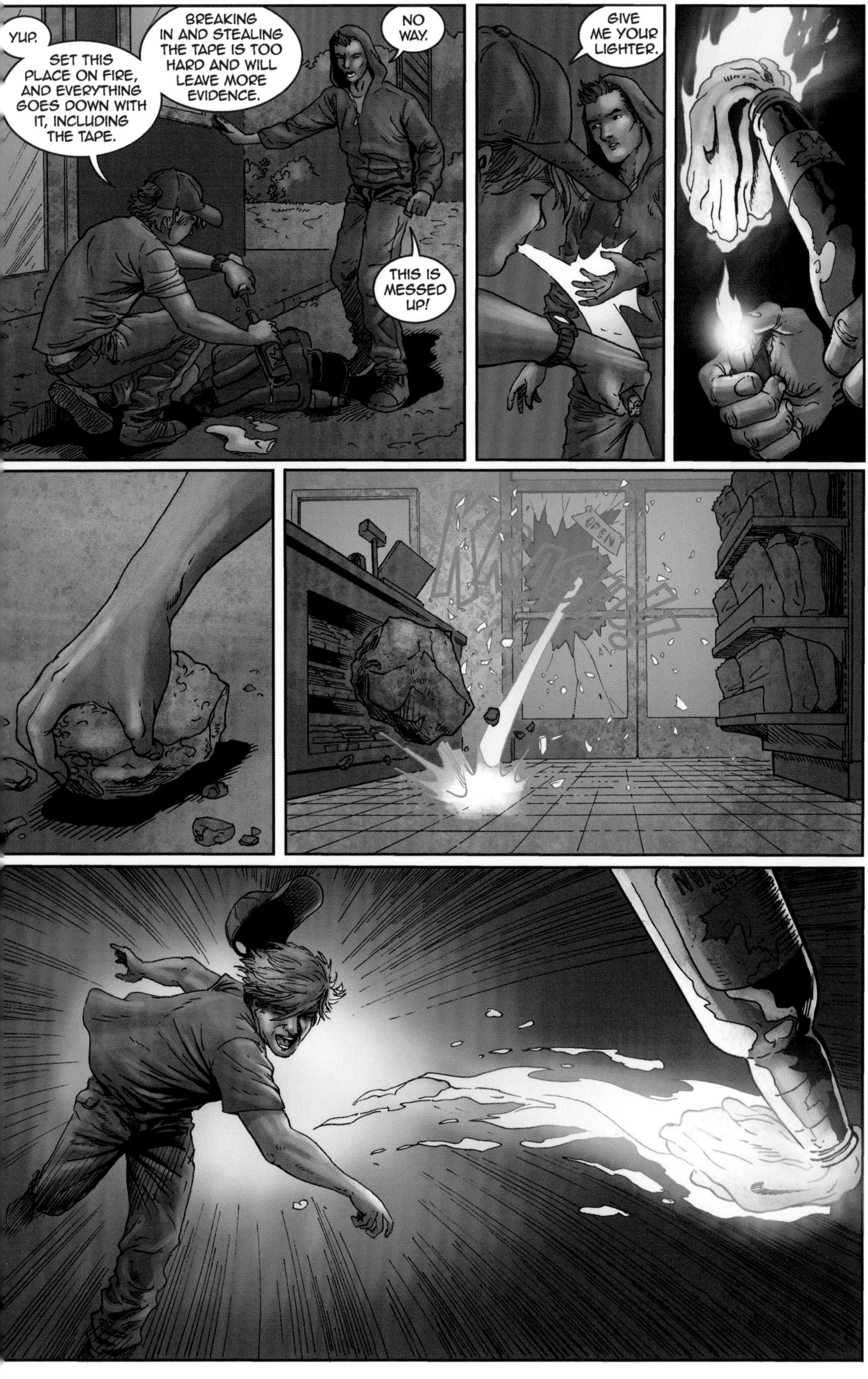
YUP.
SET THIS PLACE ON FIRE, AND EVERYTHING GOES DOWN WITH IT, INCLUDING THE TAPE.
BREAKING IN AND STEALING THE TAPE IS TOO HARD AND WILL LEAVE MORE EVIDENCE.
NO WAY.
THIS IS MESSED UP!
GIVE ME YOUR LIGHTER.
OPEN

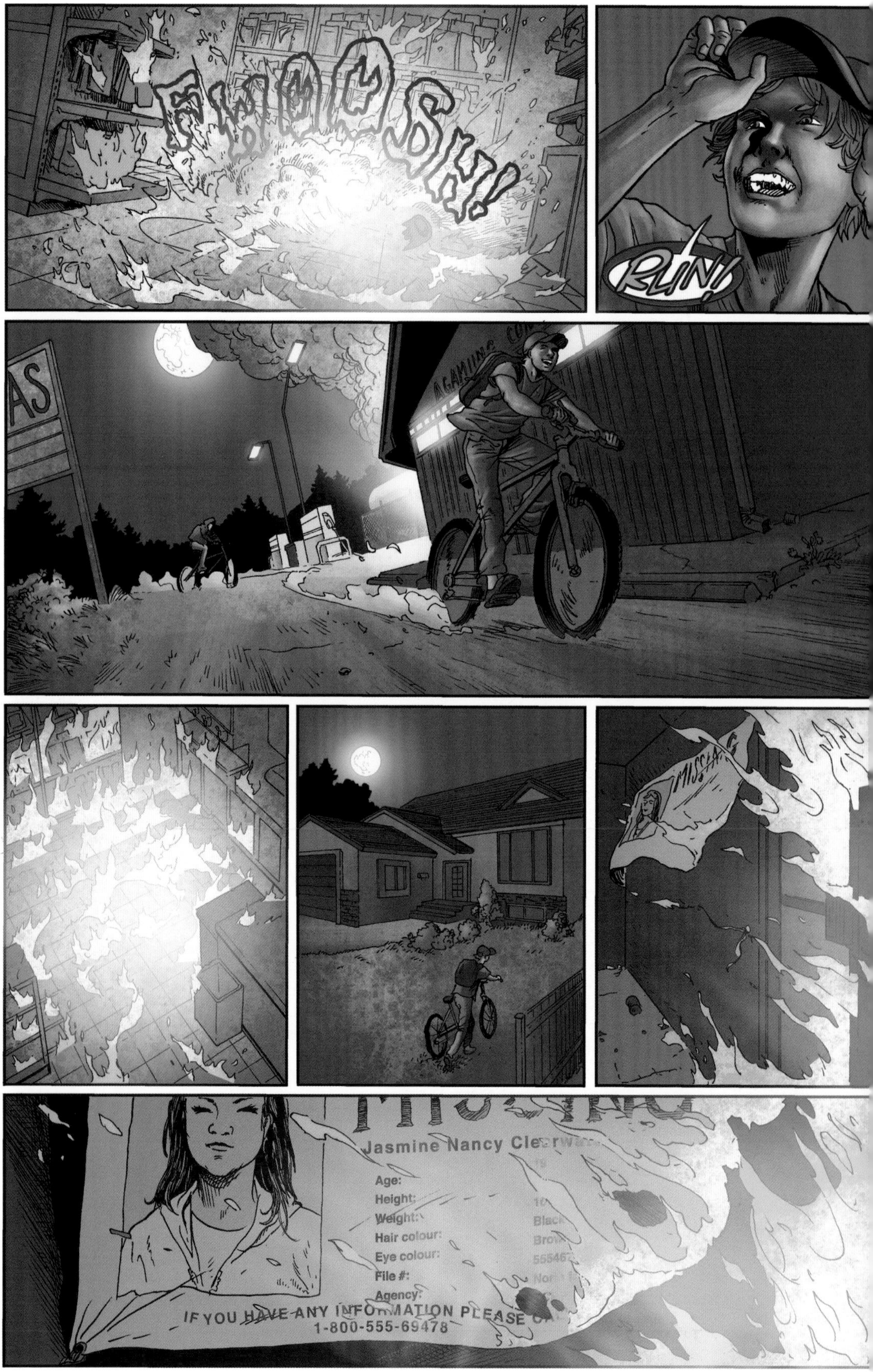
FWOOSH!!
RUN!
MISSING
Jasmine Nancy
Age:
Height:
Weight:
Hair colour:
Eye colour:
File #:
Agency:
IF YOU HAVE ANY INFORMATION PLEASE
1-800-555-69478

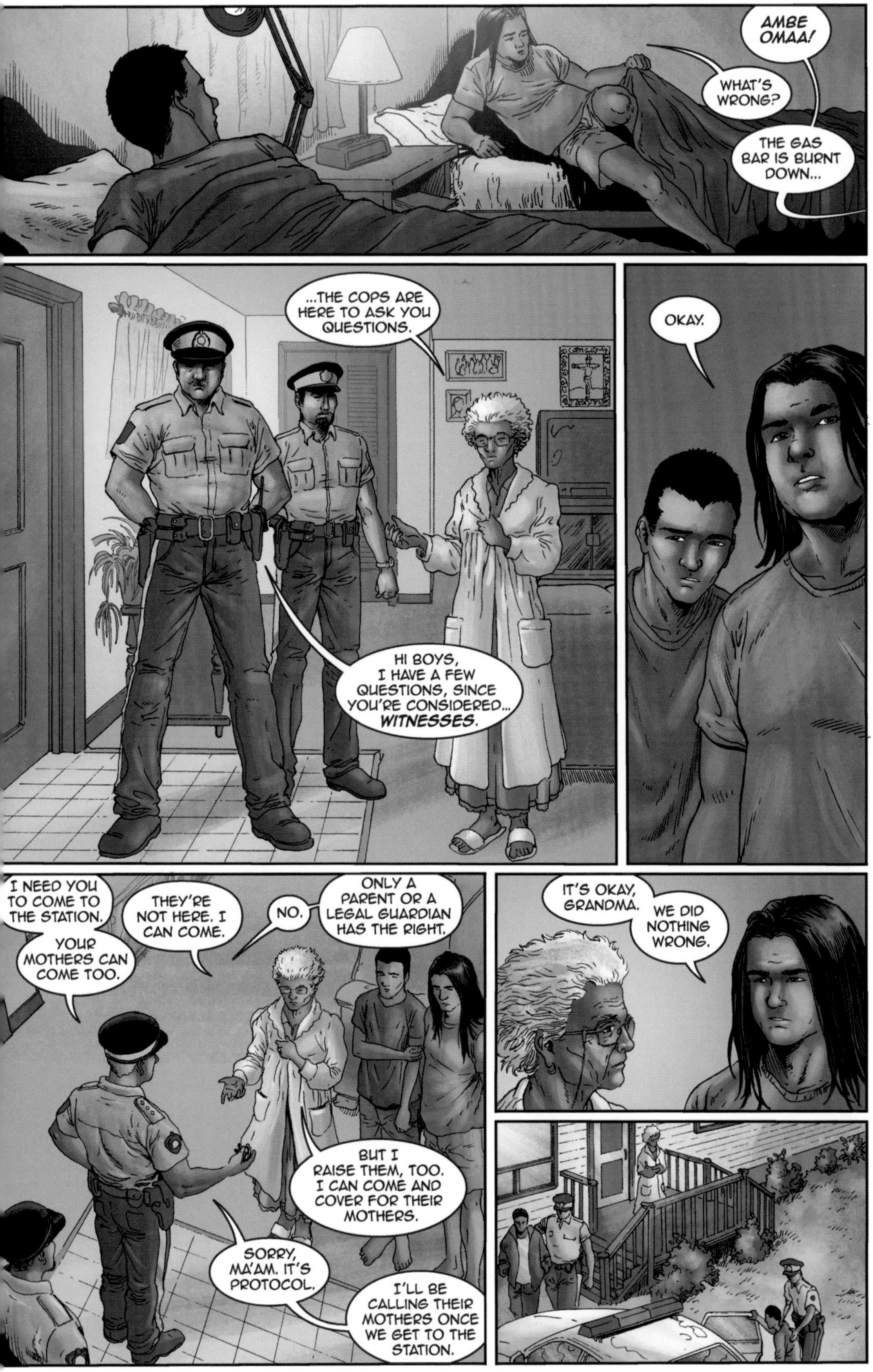
AMBE OMAA!
WHAT'S WRONG?
THE GAS BAR IS BURNT DOWN...
...THE COPS ARE HERE TO ASK YOU QUESTIONS.
HI BOYS, I HAVE A FEW QUESTIONS, SINCE YOU'RE CONSIDERED... WITNESSES.
OKAY.
I NEED YOU TO COME TO THE STATION.
YOUR MOTHERS CAN COME TOO.
THEY'RE NOT HERE. I CAN COME.
NO.
ONLY A PARENT OR A LEGAL GUARDIAN HAS THE RIGHT.
BUT I RAISE THEM, TOO. I CAN COME AND COVER FOR THEIR MOTHERS.
SORRY, MA'AM. IT'S PROTOCOL.
I'LL BE CALLING THEIR MOTHERS ONCE WE GET TO THE STATION.
IT'S OKAY, GRANDMA.
WE DID NOTHING WRONG.

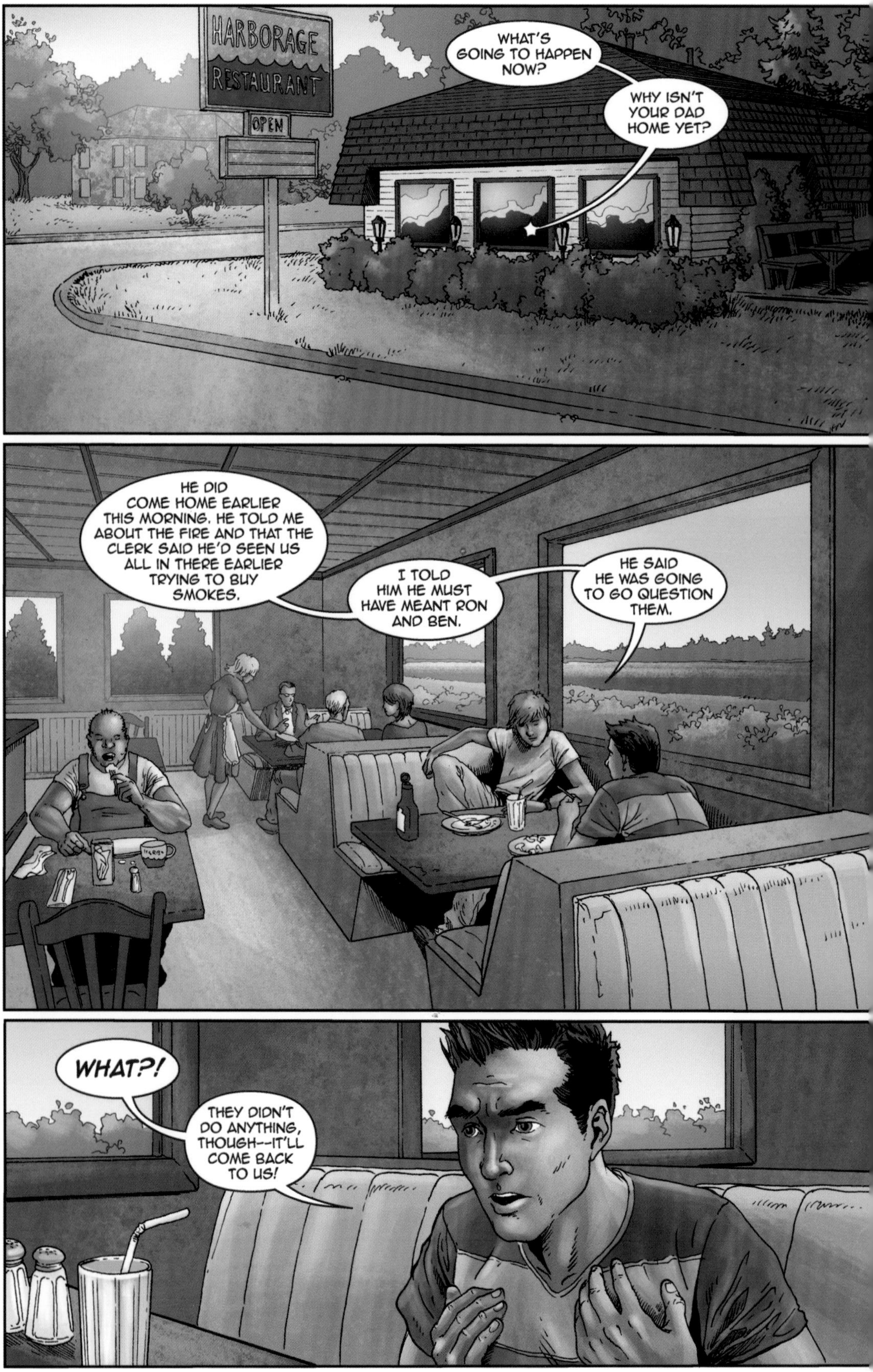

HARBORAGE
RESTAURANT
OPEN
WHAT'S GOING TO HAPPEN NOW?
WHY ISN'T YOUR DAD HOME YET?
HE DID COME HOME EARLIER THIS MORNING. HE TOLD ME ABOUT THE FIRE AND THAT THE CLERK SAID HE'D SEEN US ALL IN THERE EARLIER TRYING TO BUY SMOKES.
I TOLD HIM HE MUST HAVE MEANT RON AND BEN.
HE SAID HE WAS GOING TO GO QUESTION THEM.
WHAT?!
THEY DIDN'T DO ANYTHING, THOUGH--IT'LL COME BACK TO US!

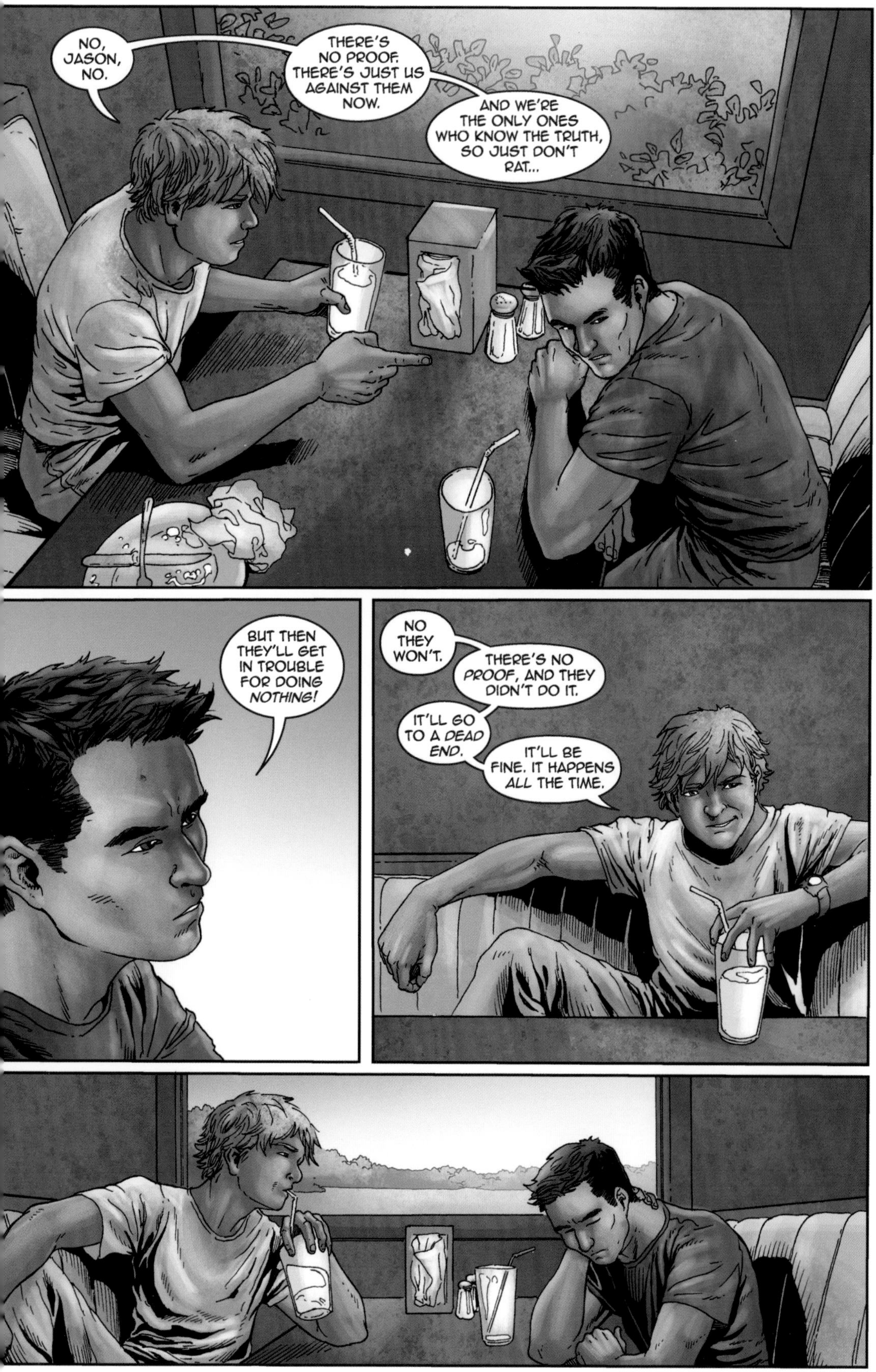
NO, JASON, NO.
THERE'S NO PROOF. THERE'S JUST US AGAINST THEM NOW.
AND WE'RE THE ONLY ONES WHO KNOW THE TRUTH, SO JUST DON'T RAT...
BUT THEN THEY'LL GET IN TROUBLE FOR DOING *NOTHING!*
NO THEY WON'T.
THERE'S NO *PROOF*, AND THEY DIDN'T DO IT.
IT'LL GO TO A *DEAD* END.
IT'LL BE FINE. IT HAPPENS *ALL* THE TIME.

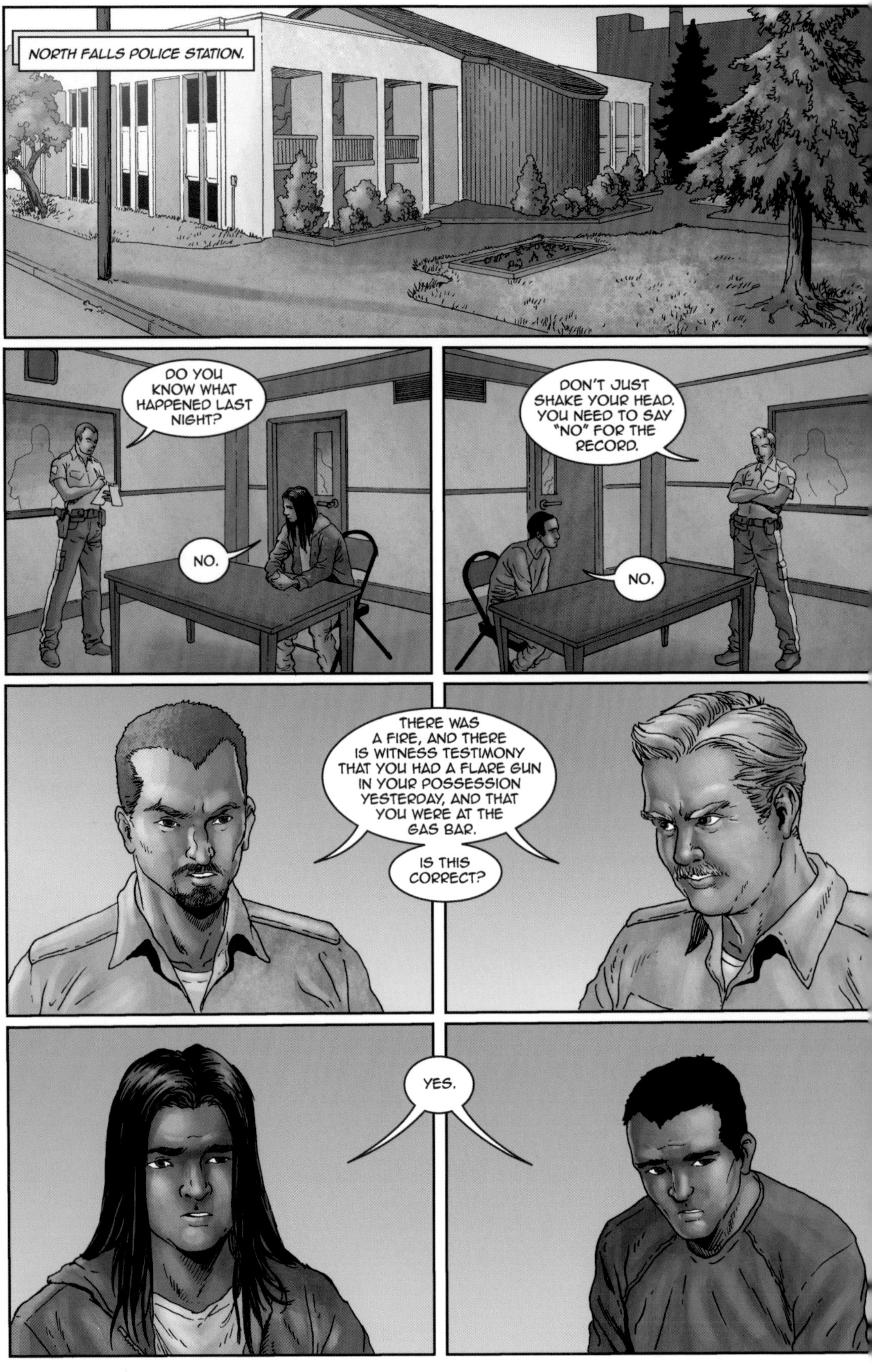
NORTH FALLS POLICE STATION.
DO YOU KNOW WHAT HAPPENED LAST NIGHT?
NO.
DON'T JUST SHAKE YOUR HEAD. YOU NEED TO SAY "NO" FOR THE RECORD.
NO.
THERE WAS A FIRE, AND THERE IS WITNESS TESTIMONY THAT YOU HAD A FLARE GUN IN YOUR POSSESSION YESTERDAY, AND THAT YOU WERE AT THE GAS BAR.
IS THIS CORRECT?
YES.

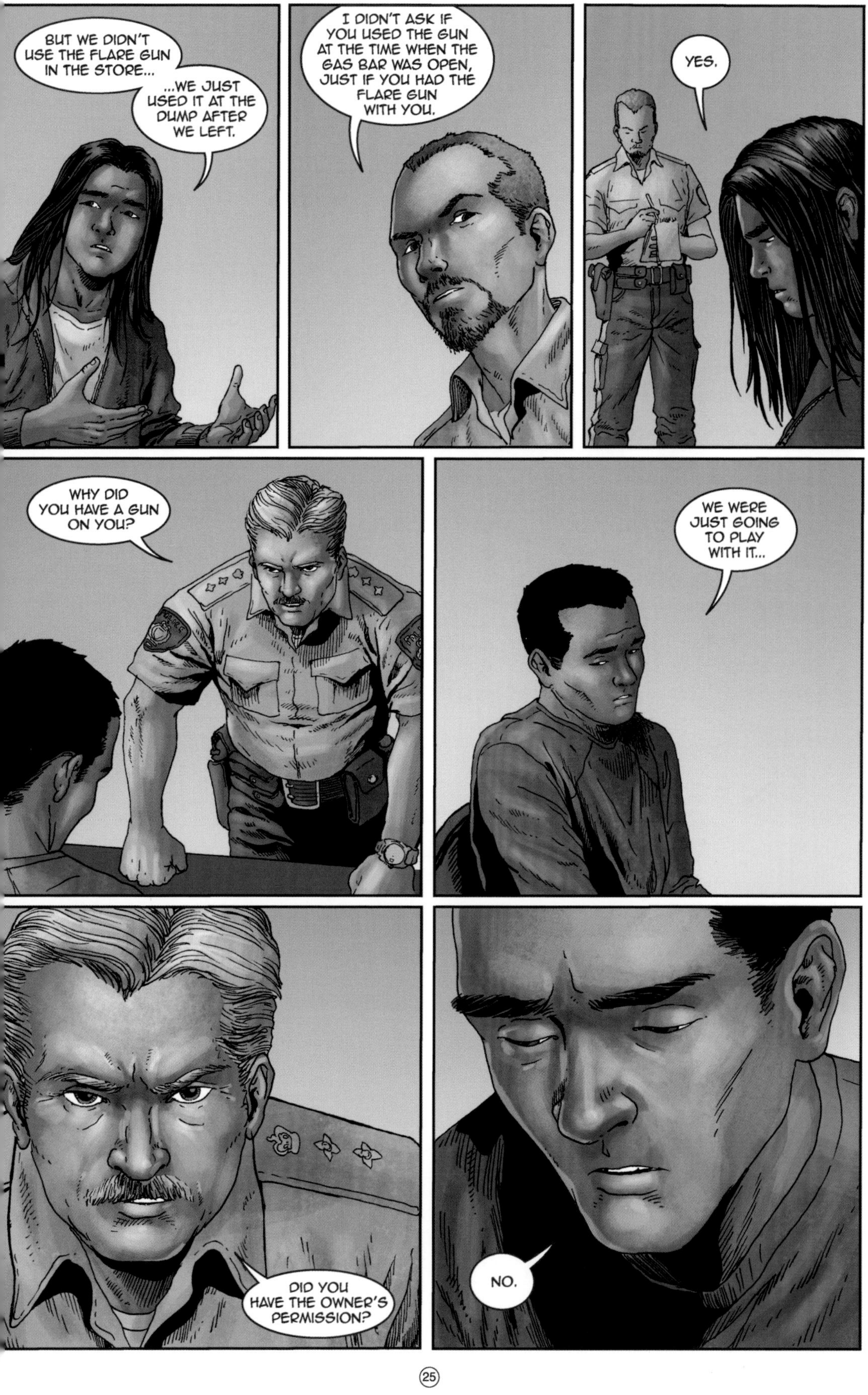

BUT WE DIDN'T USE THE FLARE GUN IN THE STORE...
...WE JUST USED IT AT THE DUMP AFTER WE LEFT.
I DIDN'T ASK IF YOU USED THE GUN AT THE TIME WHEN THE GAS BAR WAS OPEN, JUST IF YOU HAD THE FLARE GUN WITH YOU.
YES.
WHY DID YOU HAVE A GUN ON YOU?
WE WERE JUST GOING TO PLAY WITH IT...
DID YOU HAVE THE OWNER'S PERMISSION?
NO.

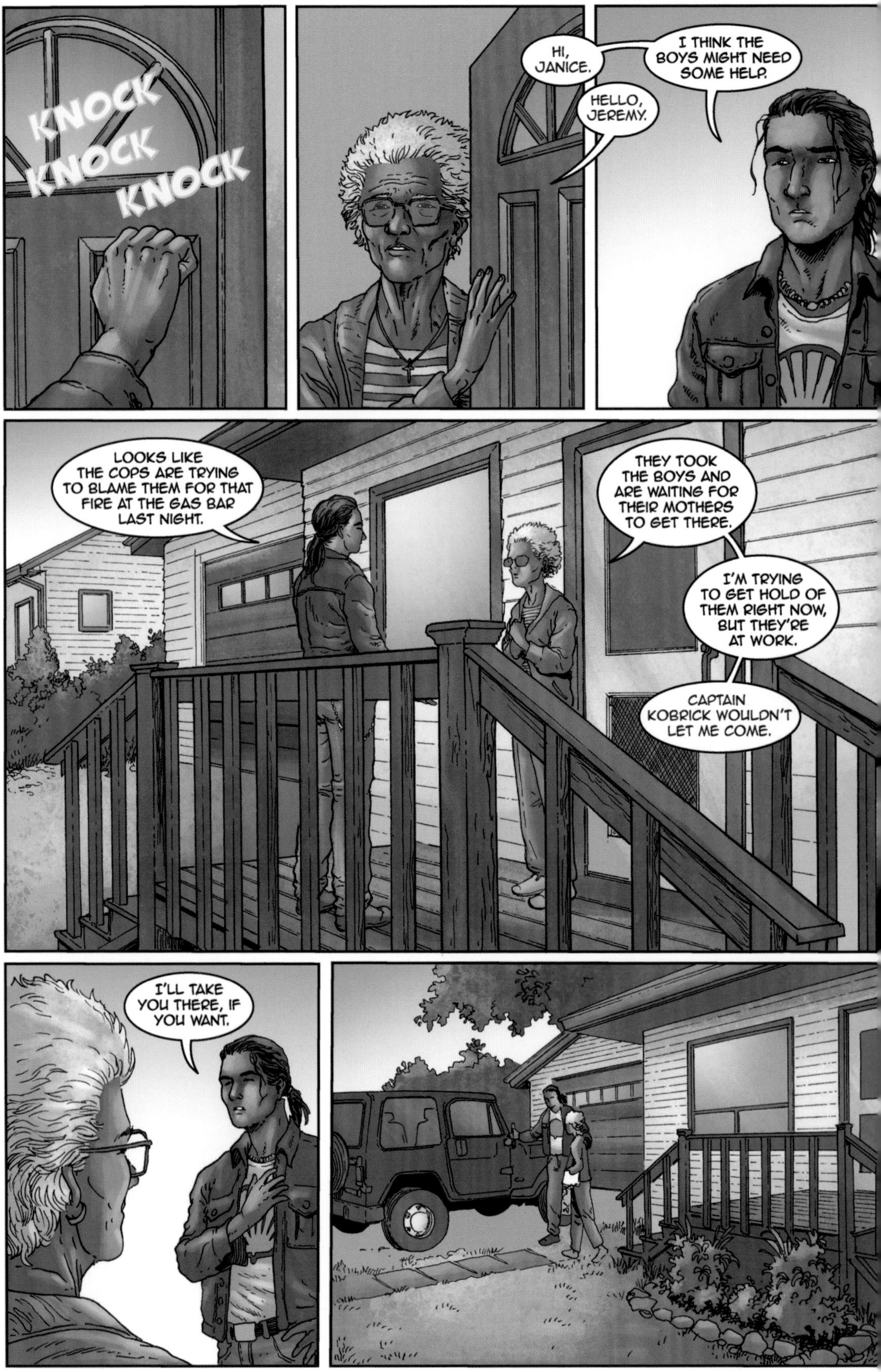
KNOCK
KNOCK
KNOCK
HI, JANICE.
HELLO, JEREMY.
I THINK THE BOYS MIGHT NEED SOME HELP.
LOOKS LIKE THE COPS ARE TRYING TO BLAME THEM FOR THAT FIRE AT THE GAS BAR LAST NIGHT.
THEY TOOK THE BOYS AND ARE WAITING FOR THEIR MOTHERS TO GET THERE.
I'M TRYING TO GET HOLD OF THEM RIGHT NOW, BUT THEY'RE AT WORK.
CAPTAIN KOBRICK WOULDN'T LET ME COME.
I'LL TAKE YOU THERE, IF YOU WANT.

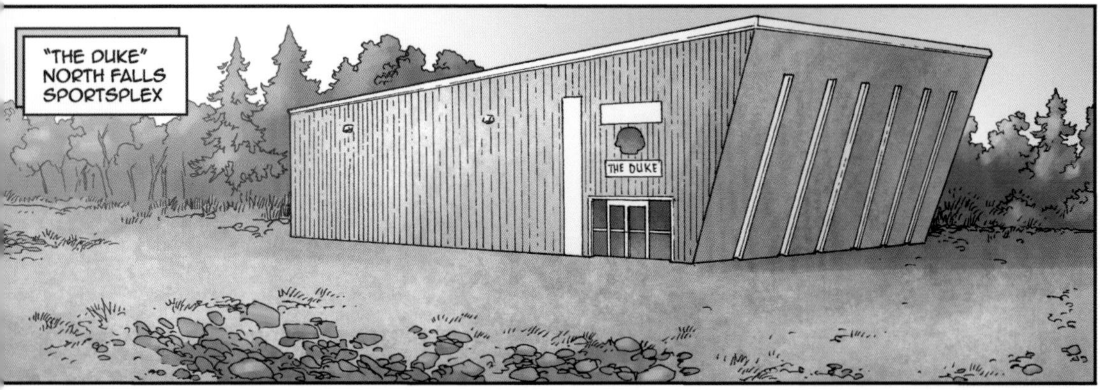
"THE DUKE" NORTH FALLS SPORTSPLEX
THE DUKE

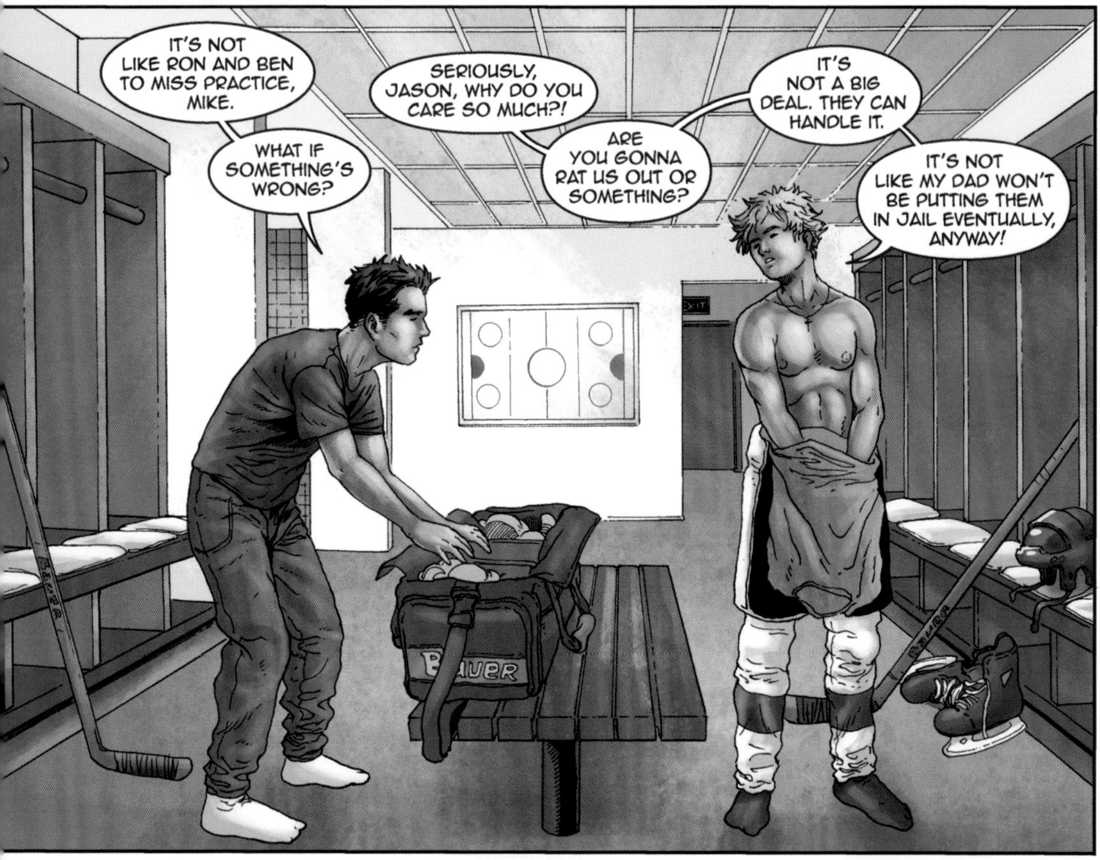
IT'S NOT LIKE RON AND BEN TO MISS PRACTICE, MIKE.
WHAT IF SOMETHING'S WRONG?
SERIOUSLY, JASON, WHY DO YOU CARE SO MUCH?!
ARE YOU GONNA RAT US OUT OR SOMETHING?
IT'S NOT A BIG DEAL. THEY CAN HANDLE IT.
IT'S NOT LIKE MY DAD WON'T BE PUTTING THEM IN JAIL EVENTUALLY, ANYWAY!
BAUER

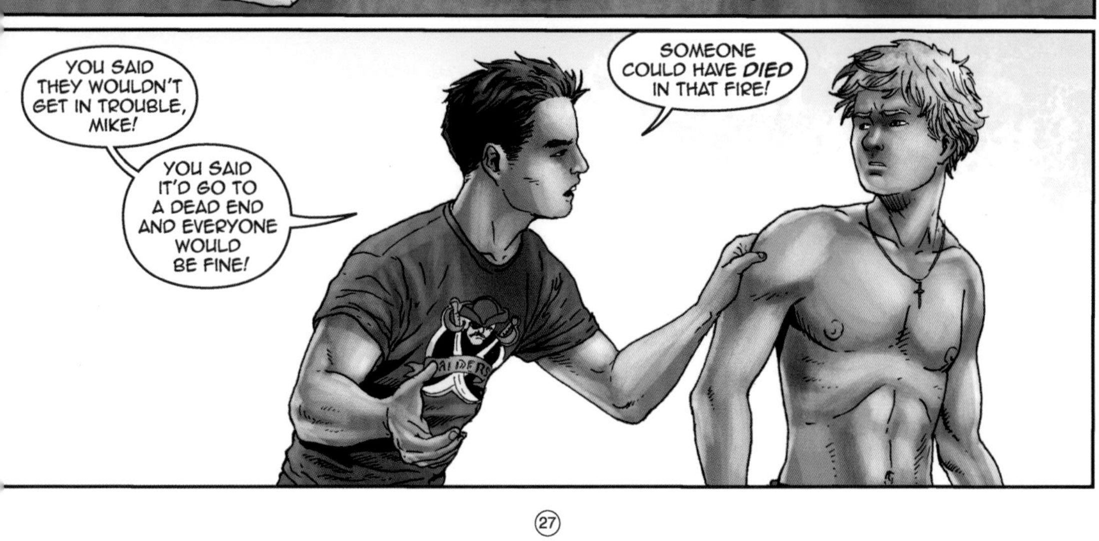
YOU SAID THEY WOULDN'T GET IN TROUBLE, MIKE!
YOU SAID IT'D GO TO A DEAD END AND EVERYONE WOULD BE FINE!
SOMEONE COULD HAVE *DIED* IN THAT FIRE!

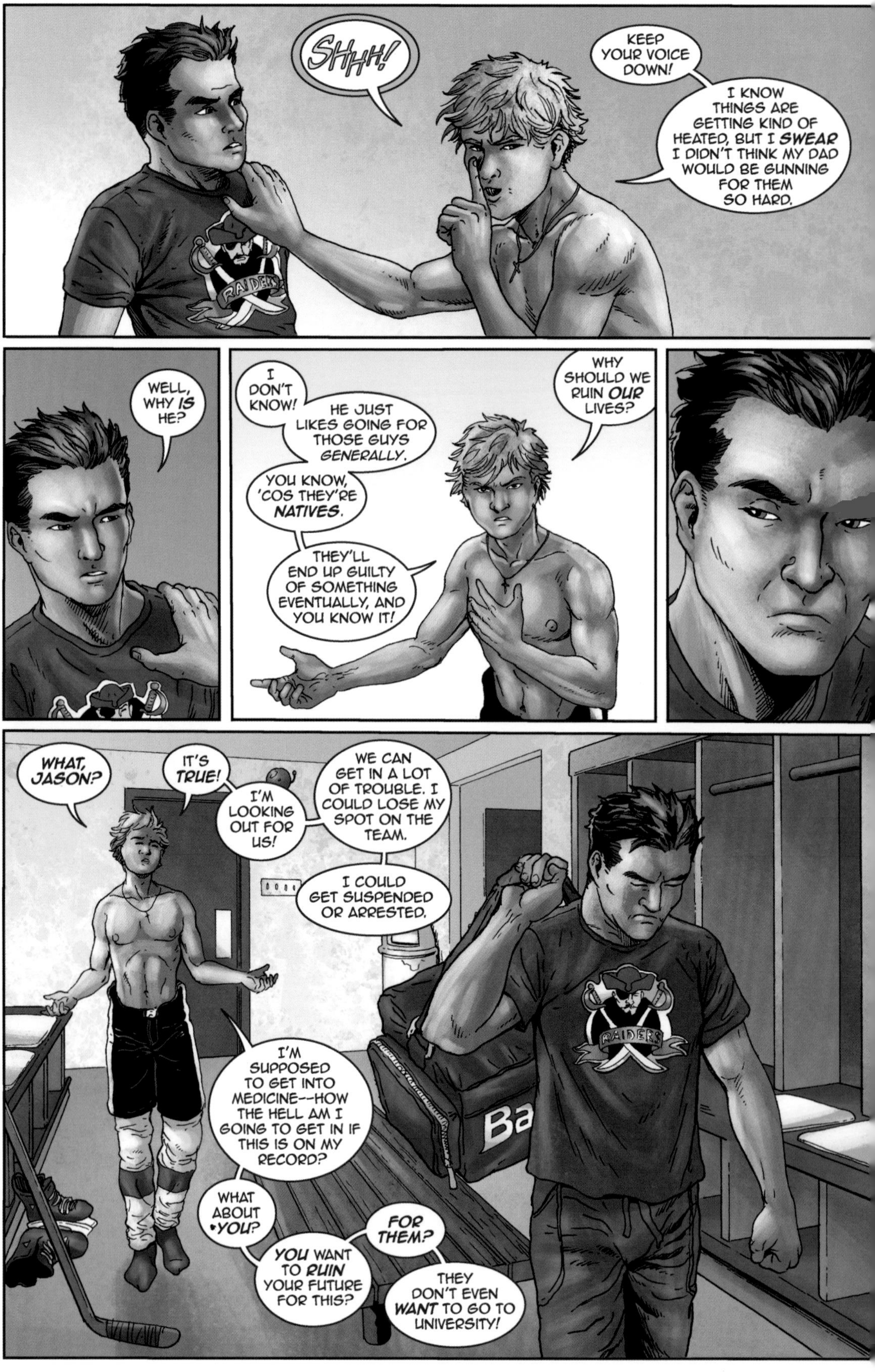
SHHH!
KEEP YOUR VOICE DOWN!
I KNOW THINGS ARE GETTING KIND OF HEATED, BUT I SWEAR I DIDN'T THINK MY DAD WOULD BE GUNNING FOR THEM SO HARD.
RAIDERS
WELL, WHY IS HE?
I DON'T KNOW!
HE JUST LIKES GOING FOR THOSE GUYS GENERALLY.
YOU KNOW, 'COS THEY'RE NATIVES.
THEY'LL END UP GUILTY OF SOMETHING EVENTUALLY, AND YOU KNOW IT!
WHY SHOULD WE RUIN OUR LIVES?
WHAT, JASON?
IT'S TRUE!
I'M LOOKING OUT FOR US!
WE CAN GET IN A LOT OF TROUBLE. I COULD LOSE MY SPOT ON THE TEAM.
I COULD GET SUSPENDED OR ARRESTED.
I'M SUPPOSED TO GET INTO MEDICINE--HOW THE HELL AM I GOING TO GET IN IF THIS IS ON MY RECORD?
WHAT ABOUT YOU?
YOU WANT TO RUIN YOUR FUTURE FOR THIS?
FOR THEM?
THEY DON'T EVEN WANT TO GO TO UNIVERSITY!
RAIDERS
Ba

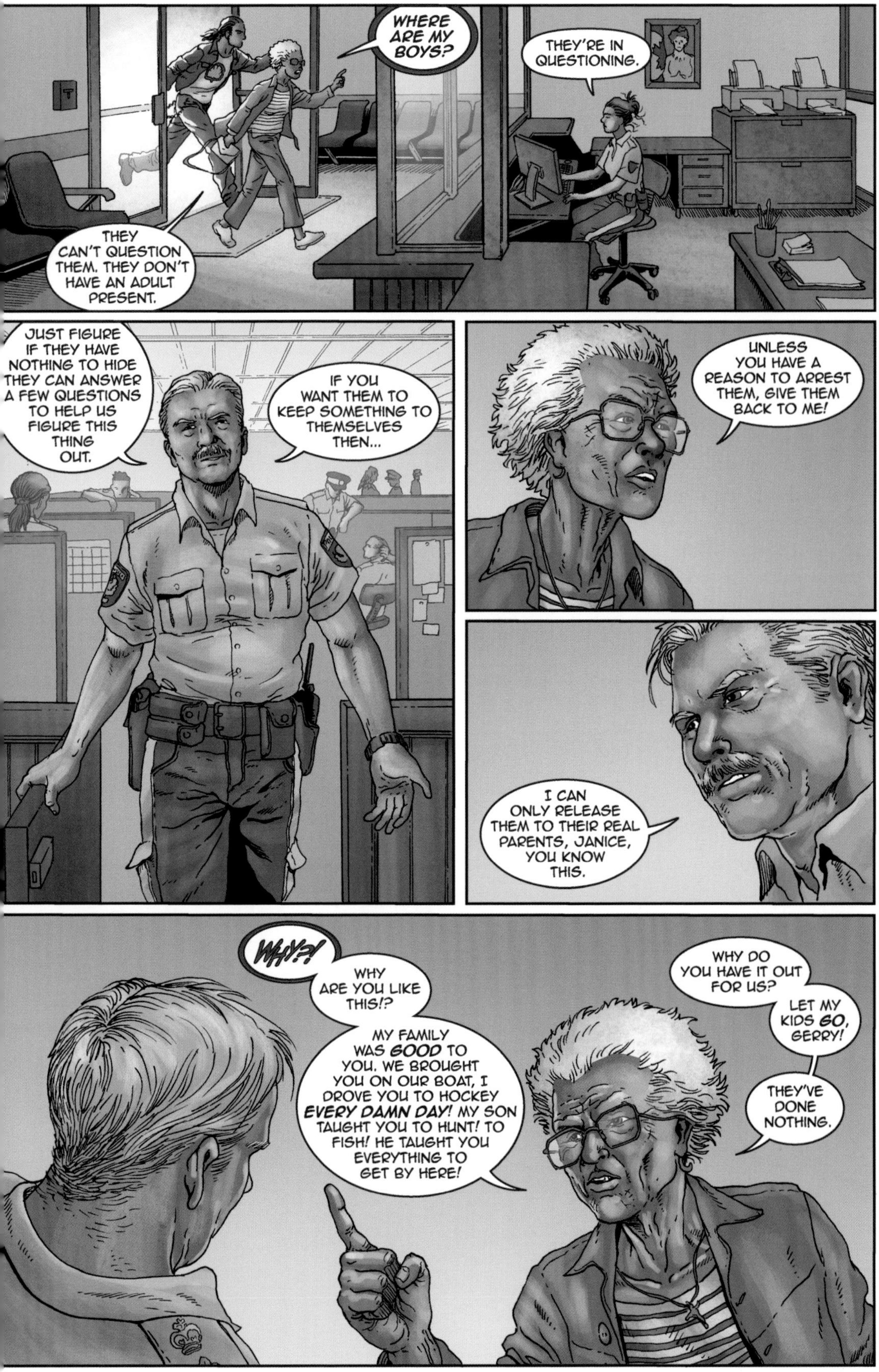

WHERE ARE MY BOYS?
THEY'RE IN QUESTIONING.
THEY CAN'T QUESTION THEM. THEY DON'T HAVE AN ADULT PRESENT.
JUST FIGURE IF THEY HAVE NOTHING TO HIDE THEY CAN ANSWER A FEW QUESTIONS TO HELP US FIGURE THIS THING OUT.
IF YOU WANT THEM TO KEEP SOMETHING TO THEMSELVES THEN...
UNLESS YOU HAVE A REASON TO ARREST THEM, GIVE THEM BACK TO ME!
I CAN ONLY RELEASE THEM TO THEIR REAL PARENTS, JANICE, YOU KNOW THIS.
WHY?!
WHY ARE YOU LIKE THIS!?
MY FAMILY WAS GOOD TO YOU. WE BROUGHT YOU ON OUR BOAT, I DROVE YOU TO HOCKEY EVERY DAMN DAY! MY SON TAUGHT YOU TO HUNT! TO FISH! HE TAUGHT YOU EVERYTHING TO GET BY HERE!
WHY DO YOU HAVE IT OUT FOR US?
LET MY KIDS GO, GERRY!
THEY'VE DONE NOTHING.

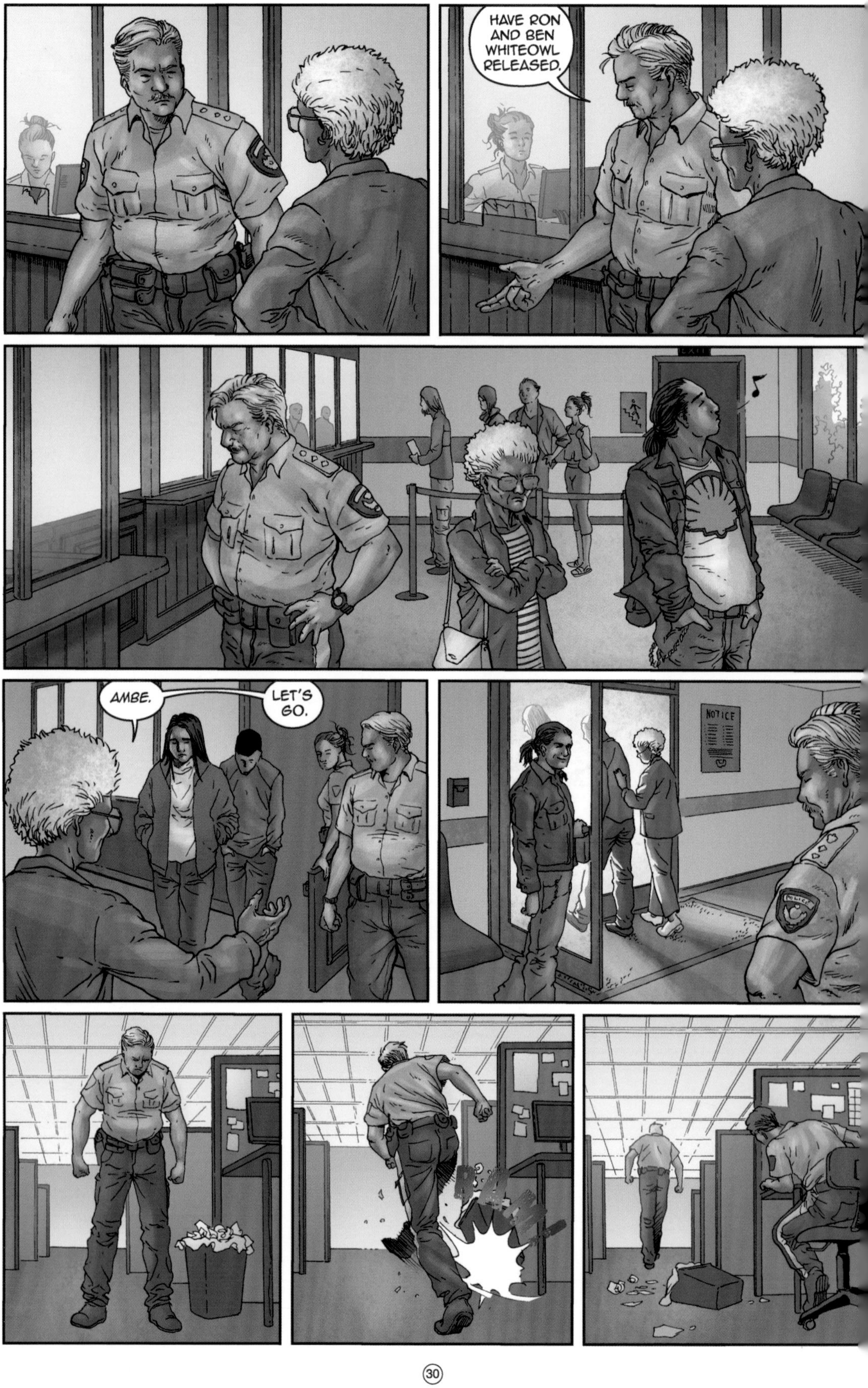
HAVE RON AND BEN WHITEOWL RELEASED.
EXIT
AMBE.
LET'S GO.
NOTICE
POLICE

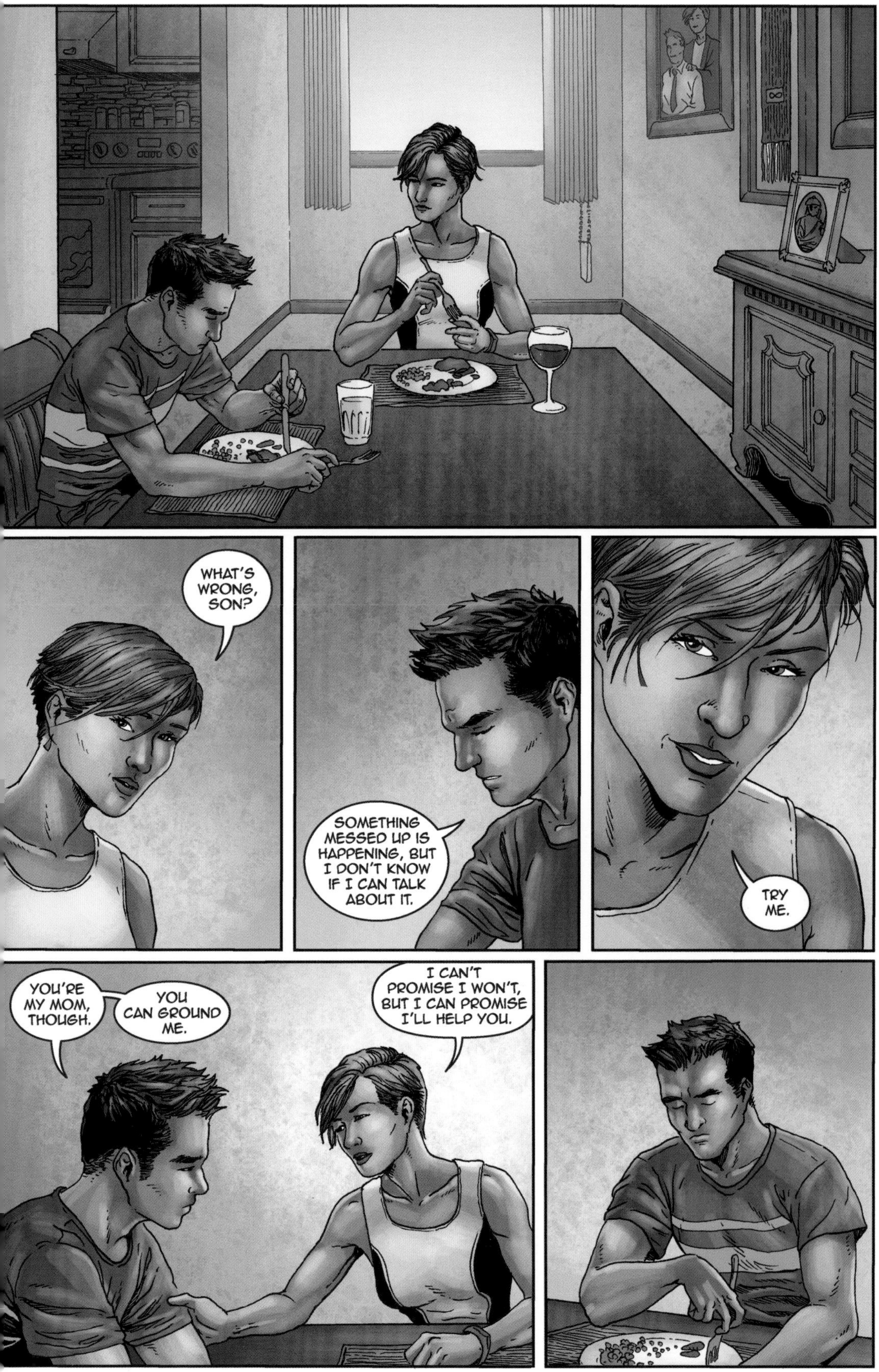
WHAT'S WRONG, SON?
SOMETHING MESSED UP IS HAPPENING, BUT I DON'T KNOW IF I CAN TALK ABOUT IT.
TRY ME.
YOU CAN GROUND ME.
YOU'RE MY MOM, THOUGH.
I CAN'T PROMISE I WON'T, BUT I CAN PROMISE I'LL HELP YOU.

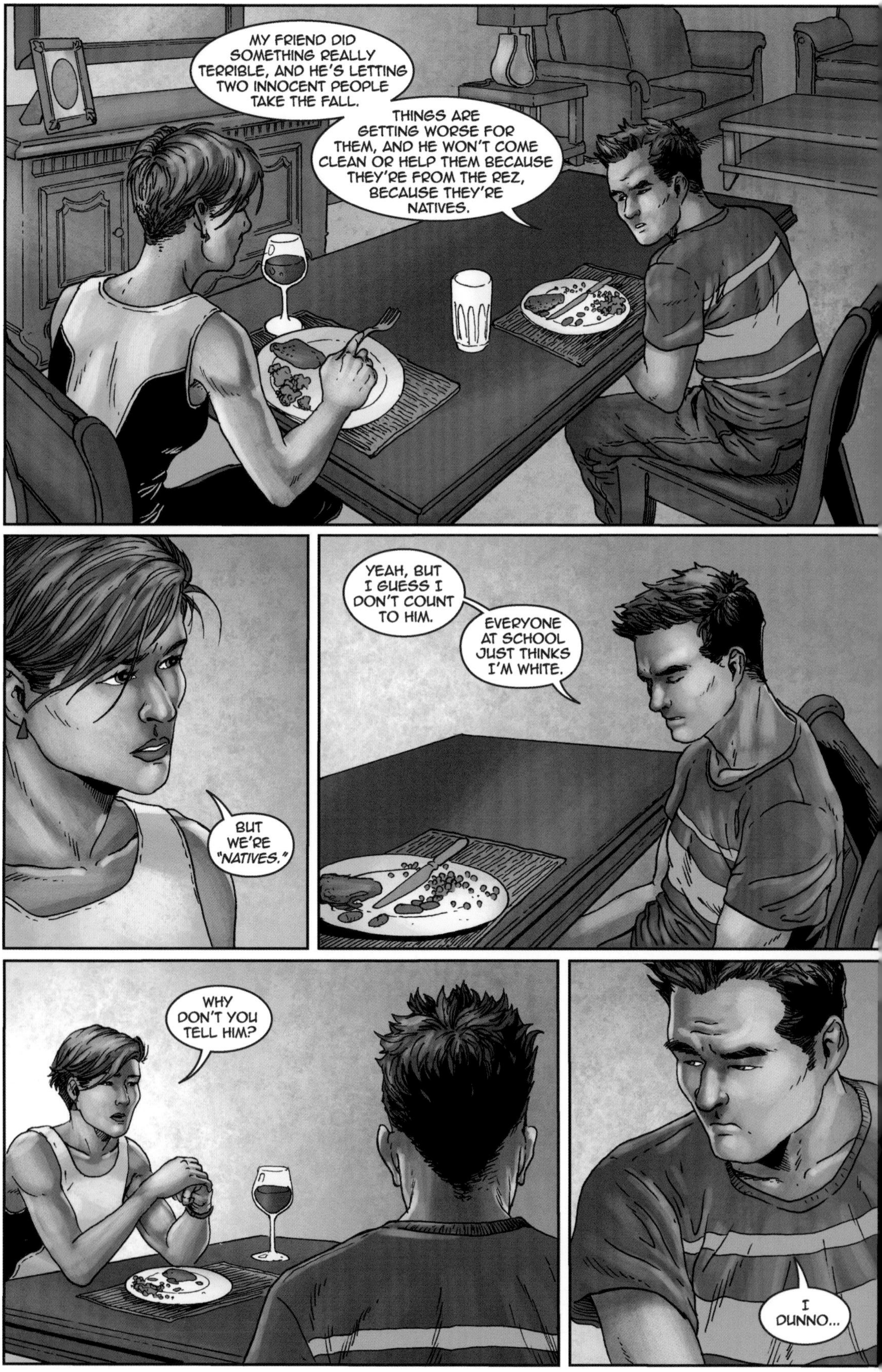

MY FRIEND DID SOMETHING REALLY TERRIBLE, AND HE'S LETTING TWO INNOCENT PEOPLE TAKE THE FALL.
THINGS ARE GETTING WORSE FOR THEM, AND HE WON'T COME CLEAN OR HELP THEM BECAUSE THEY'RE FROM THE REZ, BECAUSE THEY'RE NATIVES.
BUT WE'RE *"NATIVES."*
YEAH, BUT I GUESS I DON'T COUNT TO HIM.
EVERYONE AT SCHOOL JUST THINKS I'M WHITE.
WHY DON'T YOU TELL HIM?
I DUNNO...

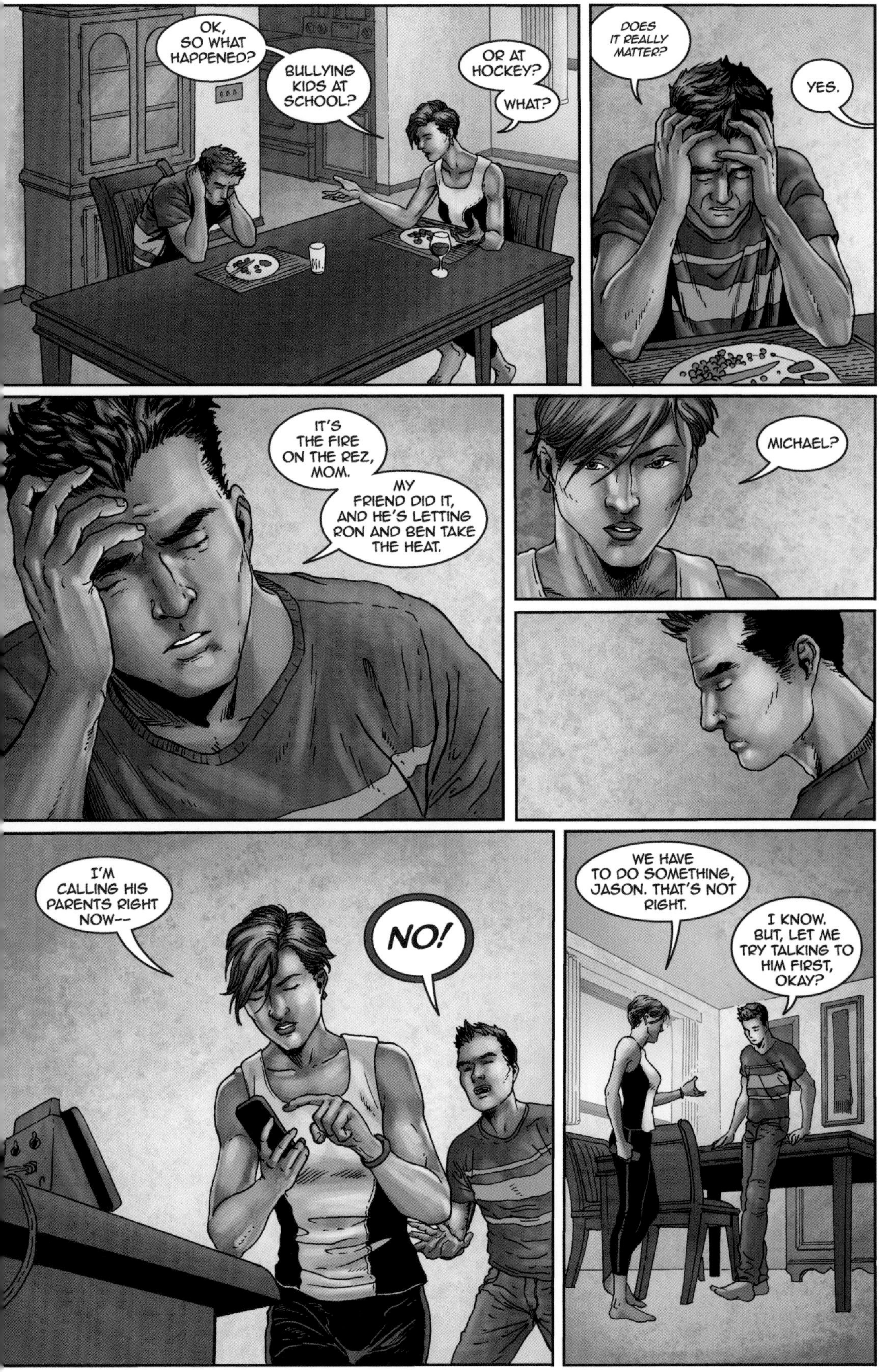
OK, SO WHAT HAPPENED?
BULLYING KIDS AT SCHOOL?
OR AT HOCKEY?
WHAT?
DOES IT REALLY MATTER?
YES.
IT'S THE FIRE ON THE REZ, MOM.
MY FRIEND DID IT, AND HE'S LETTING RON AND BEN TAKE THE HEAT.
MICHAEL?
I'M CALLING HIS PARENTS RIGHT NOW--
NO!
WE HAVE TO DO SOMETHING, JASON. THAT'S NOT RIGHT.
I KNOW. BUT, LET ME TRY TALKING TO HIM FIRST, OKAY?

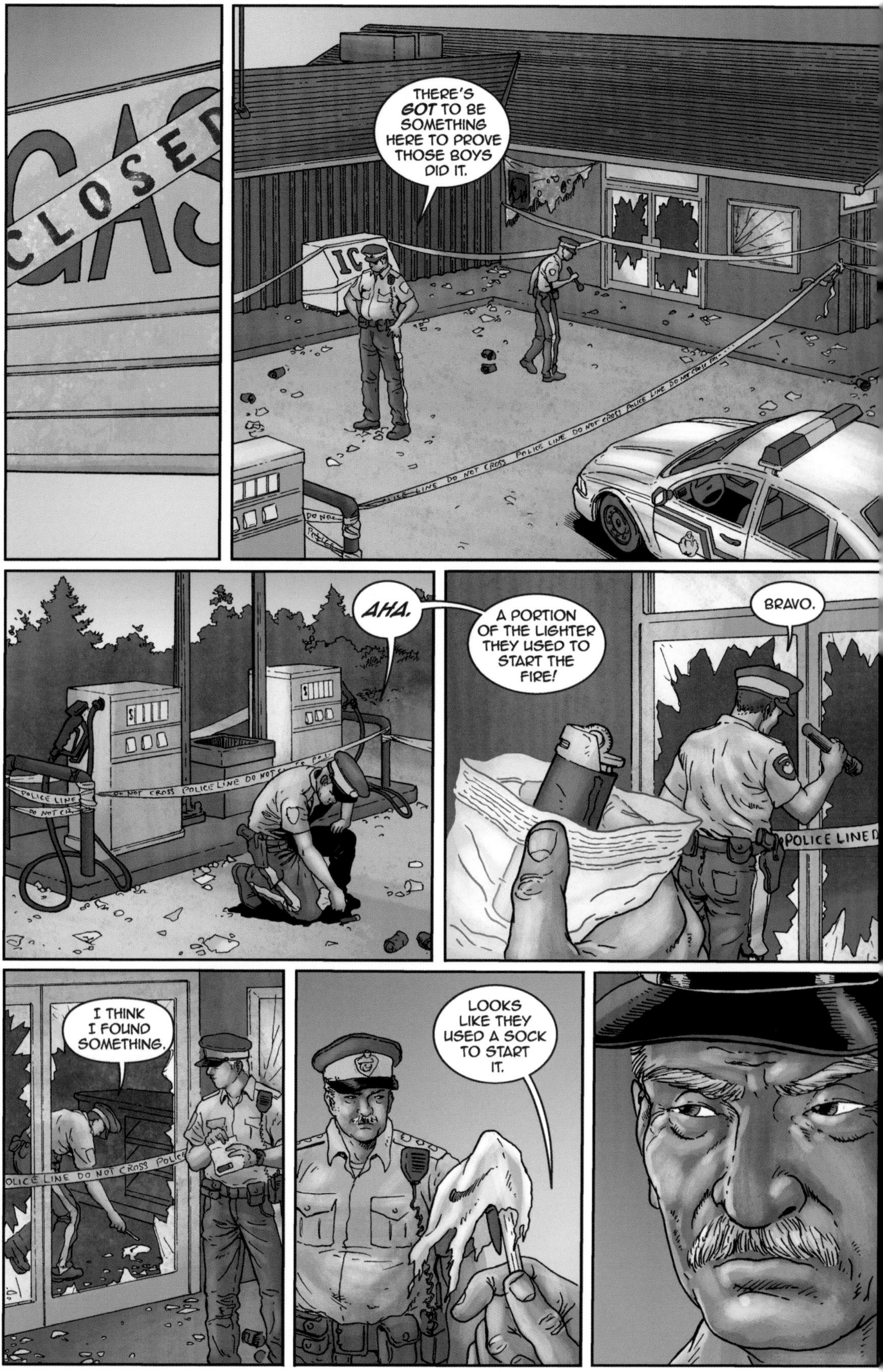
CLOSED
GAS
THERE'S *GOT* TO BE SOMETHING HERE TO PROVE THOSE BOYS DID IT.
POLICE LINE DO NOT CROSS
AHA.
A PORTION OF THE LIGHTER THEY USED TO START THE FIRE!
BRAVO.
POLICE LINE D
I THINK I FOUND SOMETHING.
POLICE LINE DO NOT CROSS POLICE
LOOKS LIKE THEY USED A SOCK TO START IT.

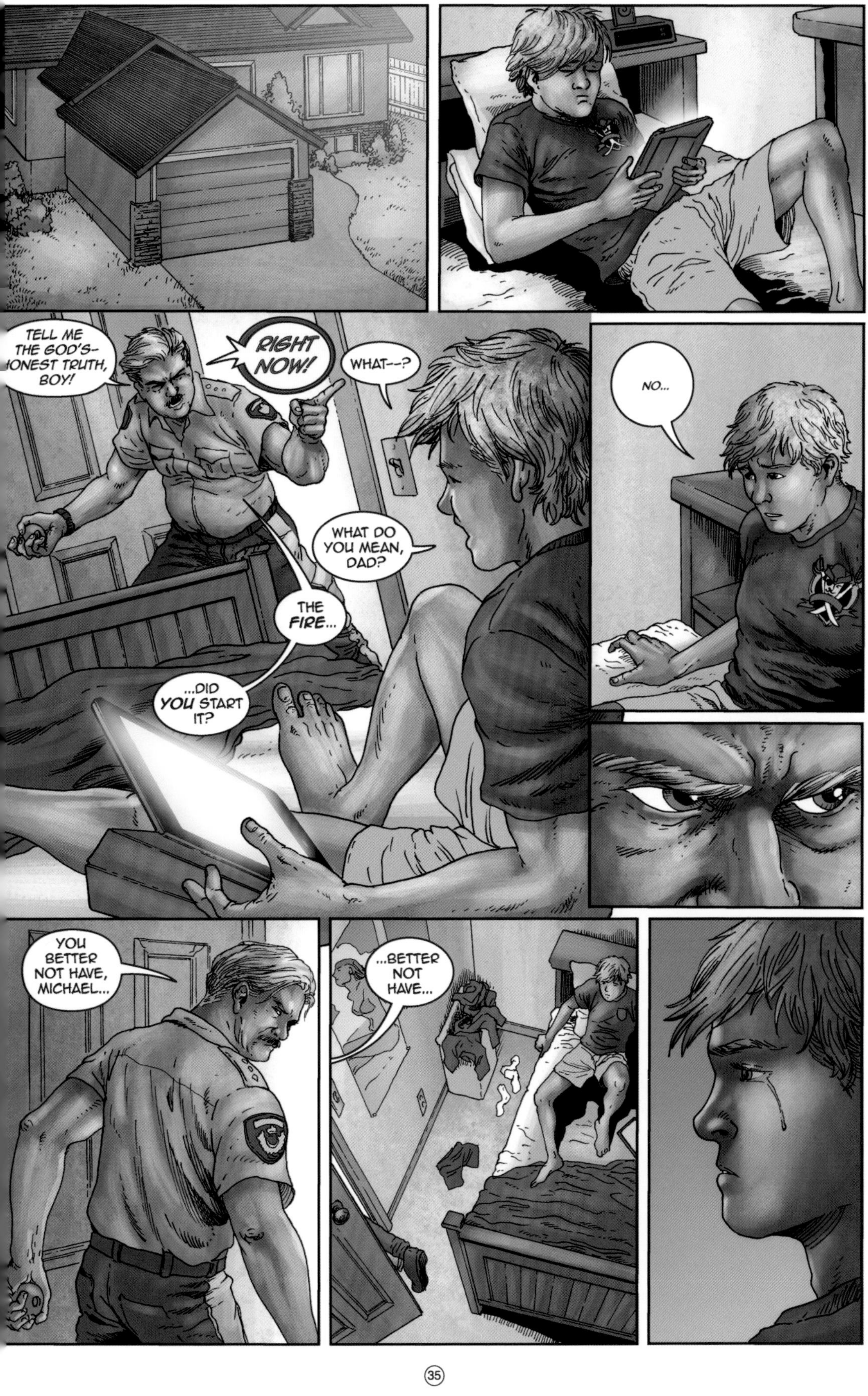

TELL ME THE GOD'S-HONEST TRUTH, BOY!
RIGHT NOW!
WHAT--?
WHAT DO YOU MEAN, DAD?
THE FIRE...
...DID YOU START IT?
NO...
YOU BETTER NOT HAVE, MICHAEL...
...BETTER NOT HAVE...

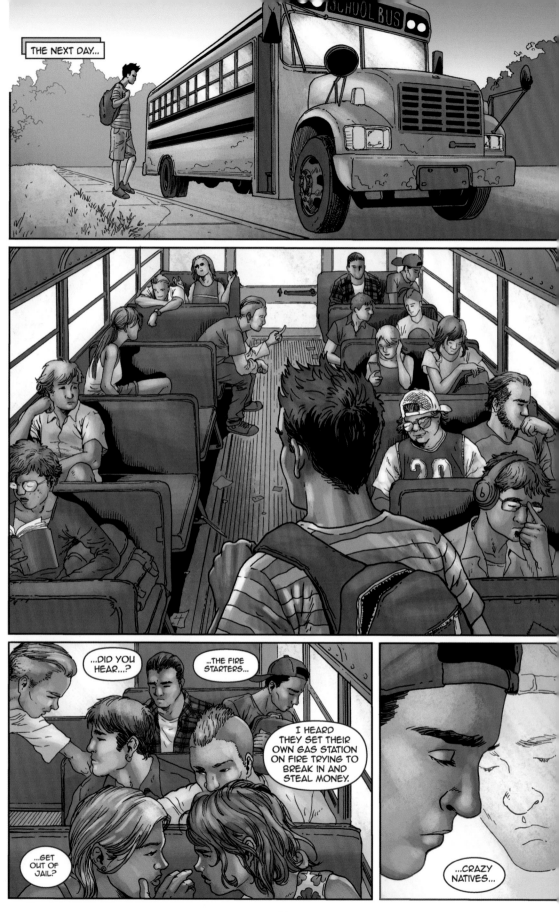

THE NEXT DAY...

...DID YOU HEAR...?

...THE FIRE STARTERS...

I HEARD THEY SET THEIR OWN GAS STATION ON FIRE TRYING TO BREAK IN AND STEAL MONEY.

...GET OUT OF JAIL?

...CRAZY NATIVES...

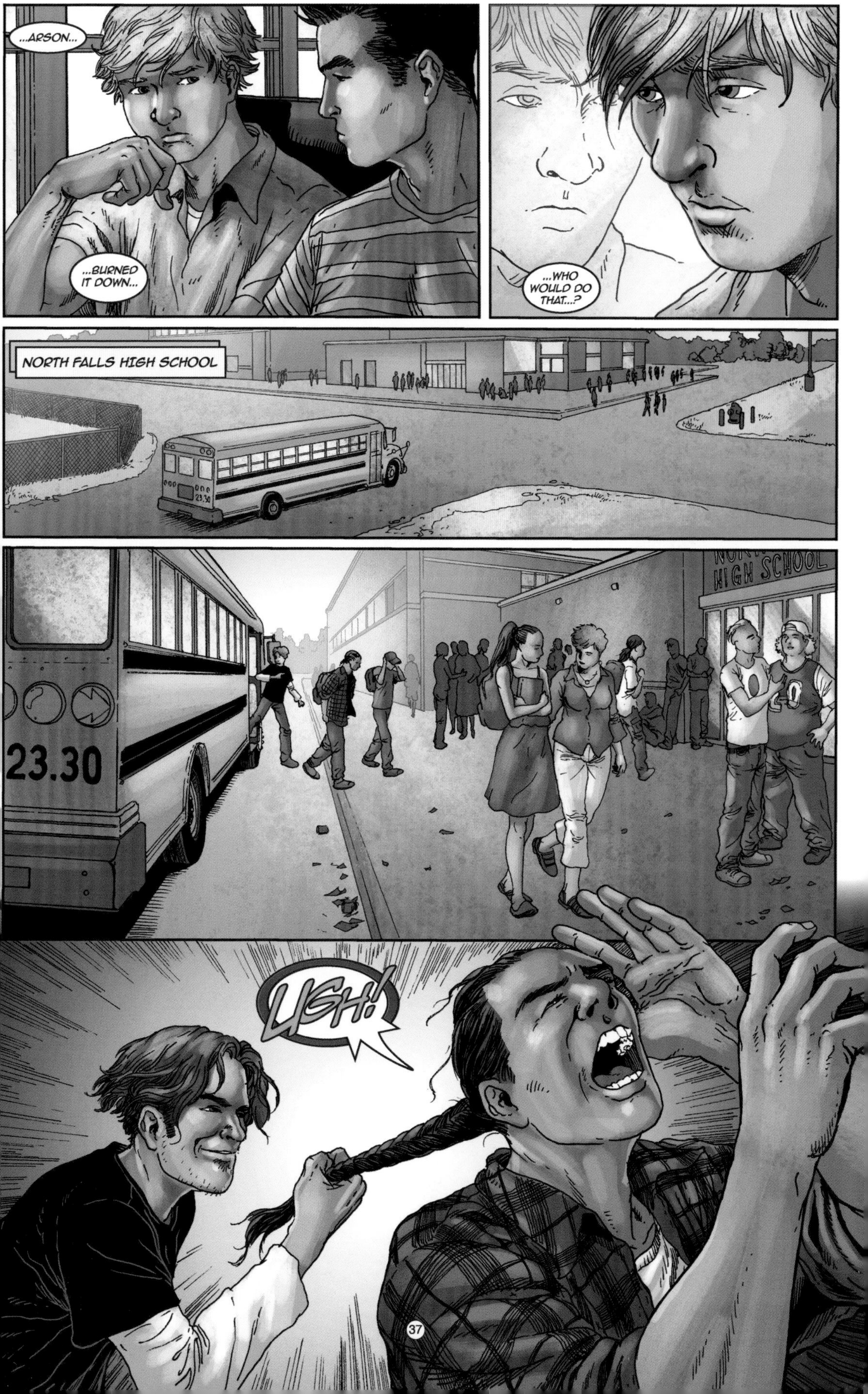

...ARSON...
...BURNED IT DOWN...
...WHO WOULD DO THAT...?
NORTH FALLS HIGH SCHOOL
23.30
HIGH SCHOOL
23.30
UGH!

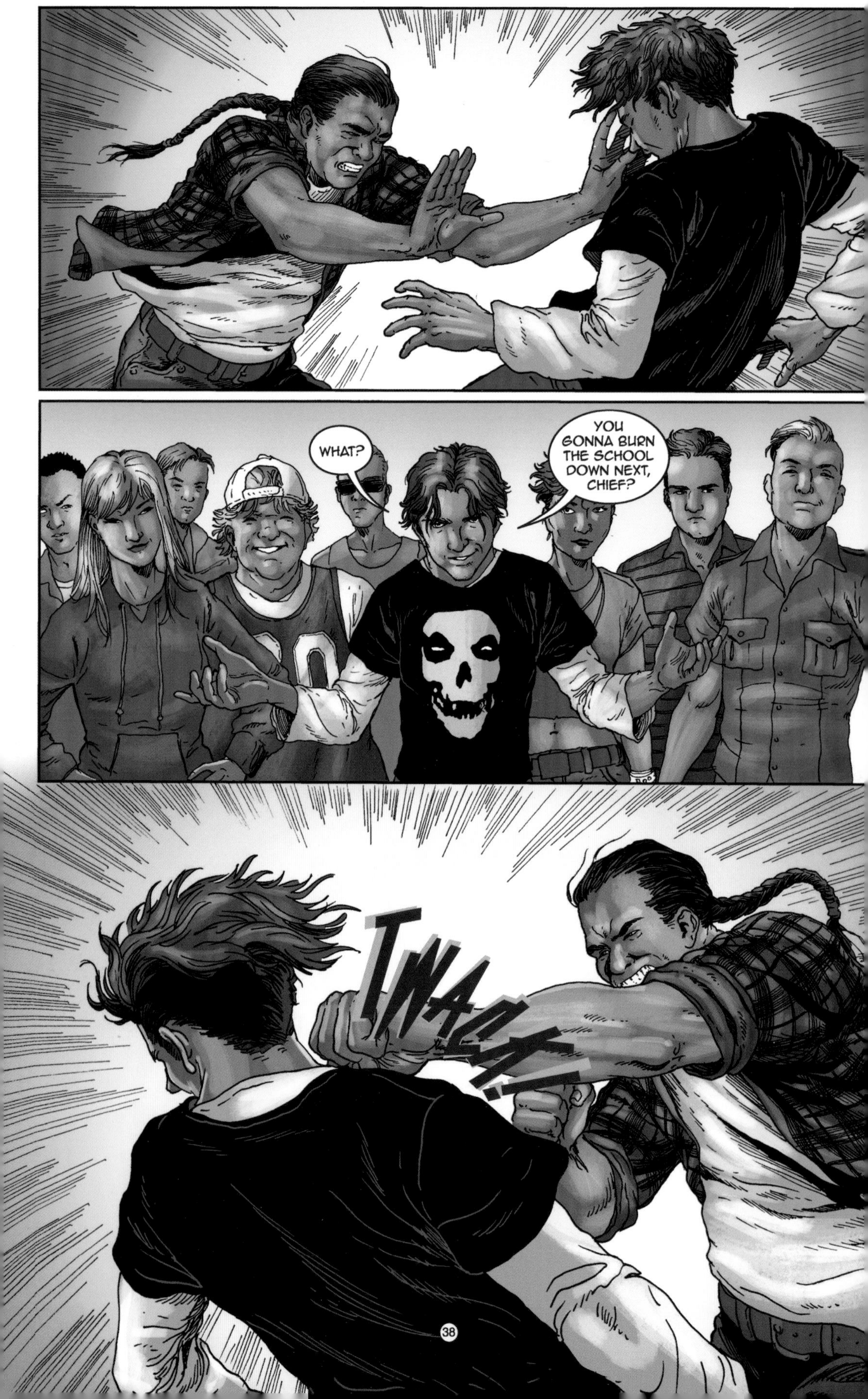
WHAT?
YOU GONNA BURN THE SCHOOL DOWN NEXT, CHIEF?
TWACK!!

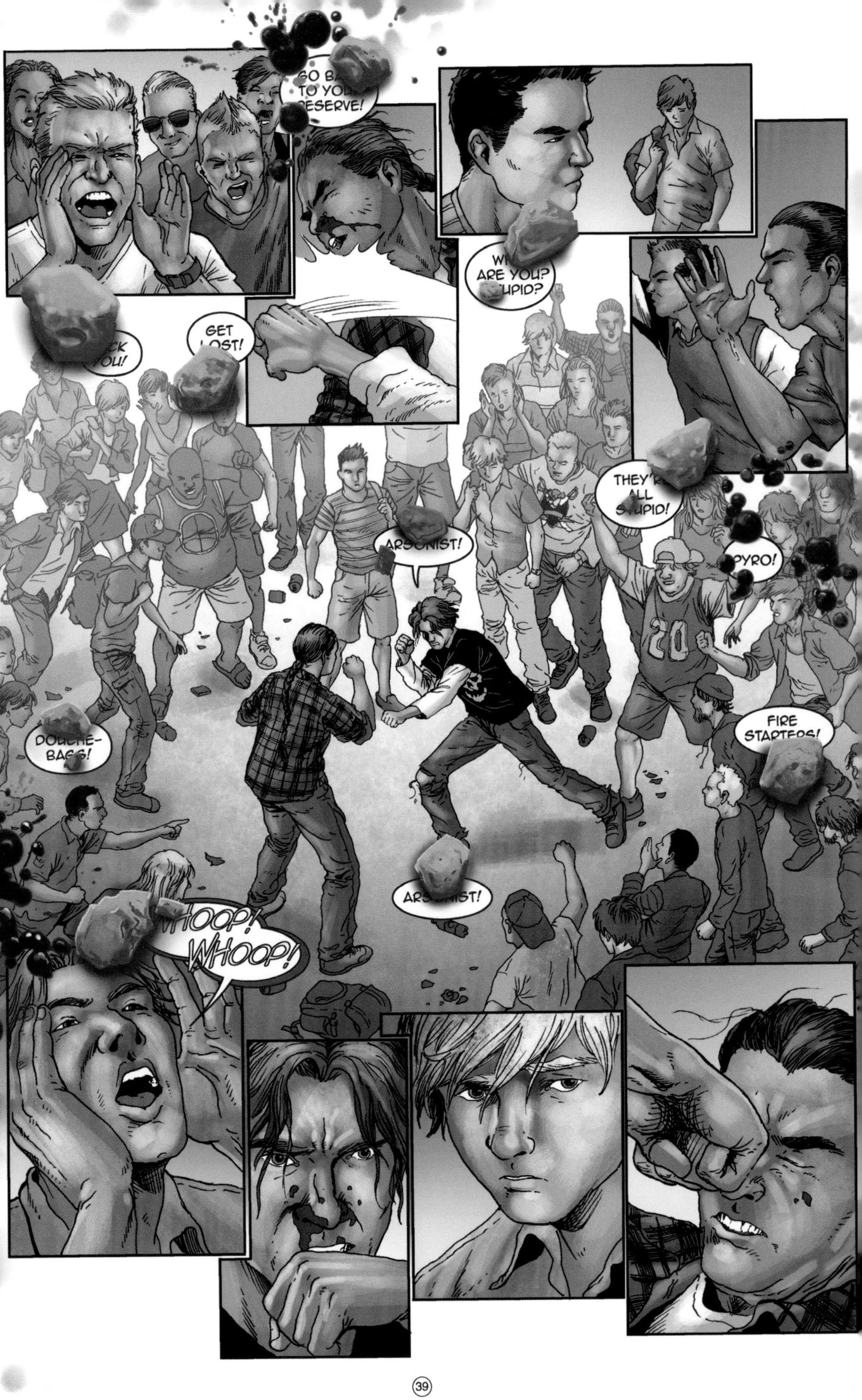
RESERVE!
ARE YOU?
GET LOST!
ARSONIST!
PYRO!
DOUCHE-BAGS!
FIRE STARTERS!
WHOOP! WHOOP!

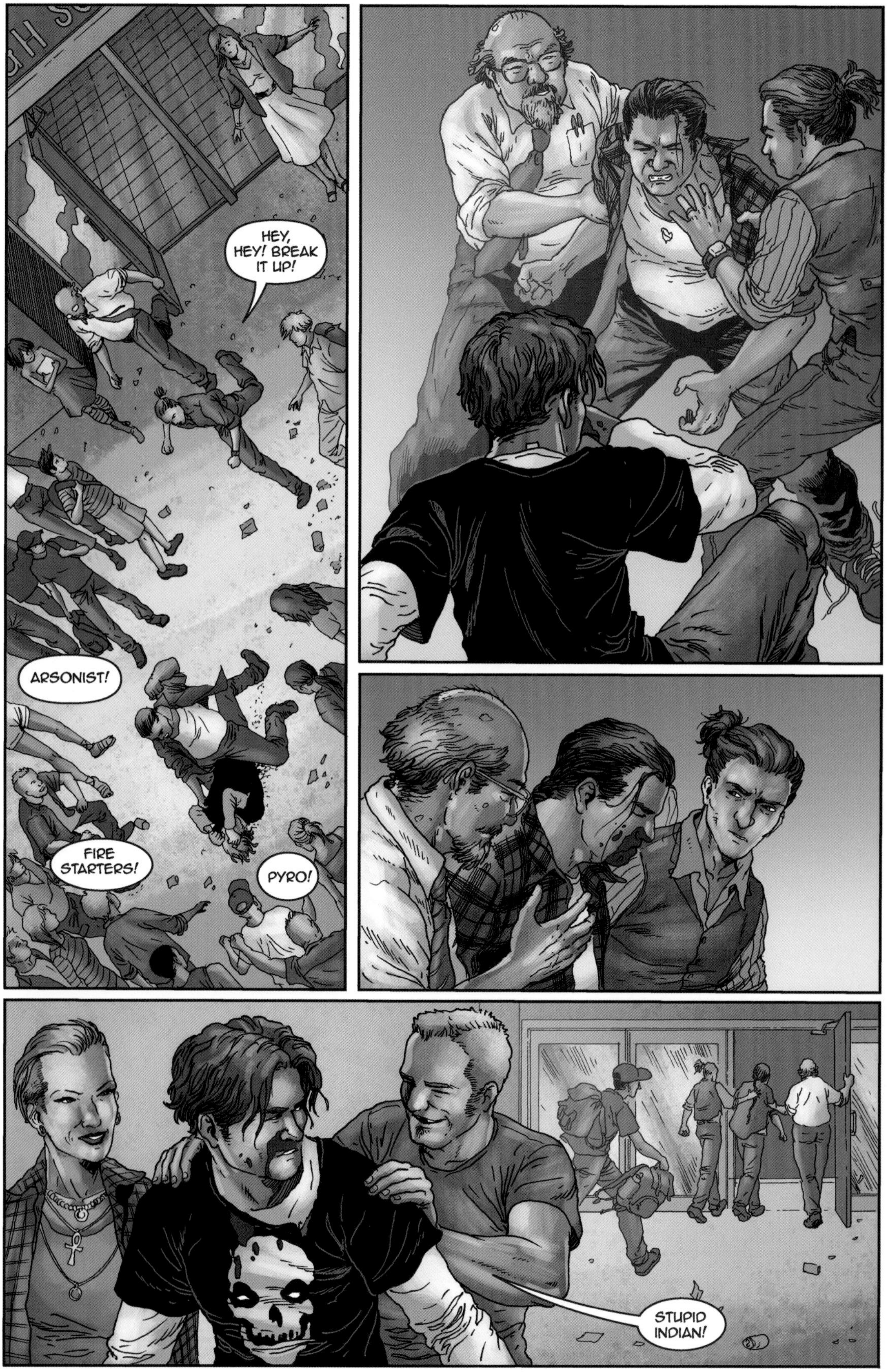
HEY, HEY! BREAK IT UP!
ARSONIST!
FIRE STARTERS!
PYRO!
STUPID INDIAN!

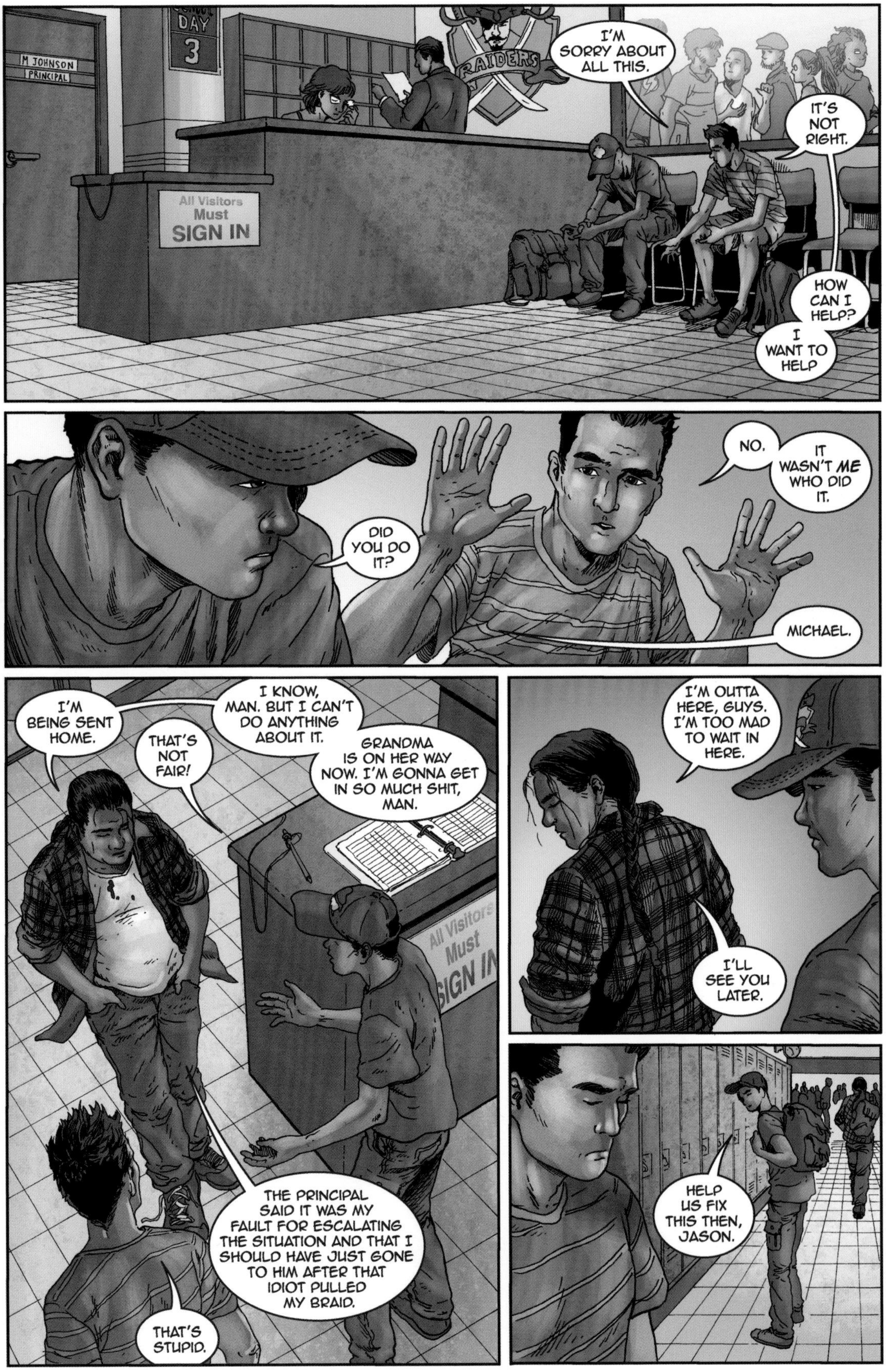
DAY
3
M JOHNSON
PRINCIPAL
RAIDERS
All Visitors Must SIGN IN
I'M SORRY ABOUT ALL THIS.
IT'S NOT RIGHT.
HOW CAN I HELP?
I WANT TO HELP
DID YOU DO IT?
NO.
IT WASN'T *ME* WHO DID IT.
MICHAEL.
I'M BEING SENT HOME.
I KNOW, MAN. BUT I CAN'T DO ANYTHING ABOUT IT.
THAT'S NOT FAIR!
GRANDMA IS ON HER WAY NOW. I'M GONNA GET IN SO MUCH SHIT, MAN.
All Visitors Must SIGN IN
THE PRINCIPAL SAID IT WAS MY FAULT FOR ESCALATING THE SITUATION AND THAT I SHOULD HAVE JUST GONE TO HIM AFTER THAT IDIOT PULLED MY BRAID.
THAT'S STUPID.
I'M OUTTA HERE, GUYS. I'M TOO MAD TO WAIT IN HERE.
I'LL SEE YOU LATER.
HELP US FIX THIS THEN, JASON.

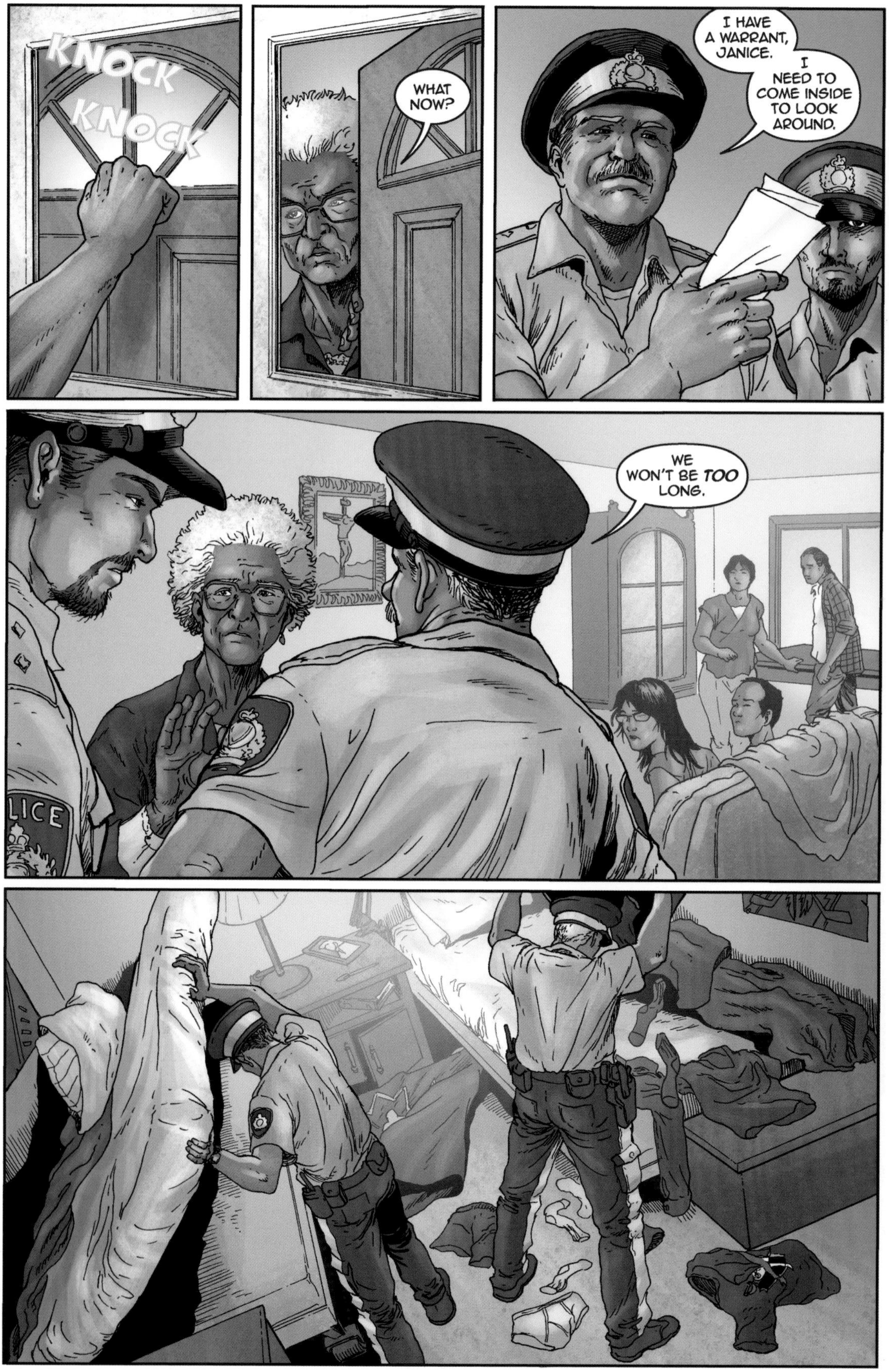
KNOCK
KNOCK
WHAT NOW?
I HAVE A WARRANT, JANICE.
I NEED TO COME INSIDE TO LOOK AROUND.
LICE
WE WON'T BE TOO LONG.

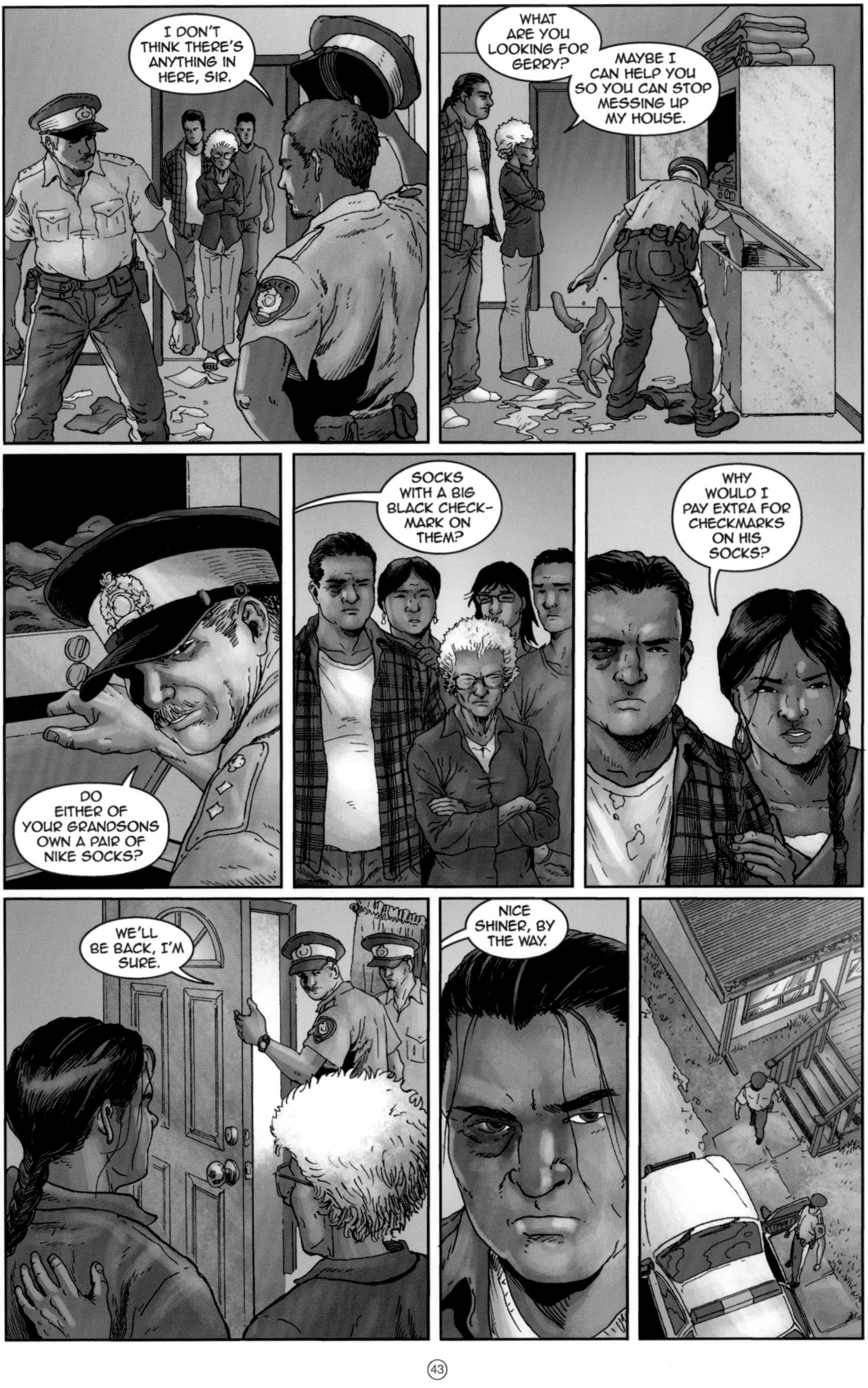
I DON'T THINK THERE'S ANYTHING IN HERE, SIR.
WHAT ARE YOU LOOKING FOR GERRY?
MAYBE I CAN HELP YOU SO YOU CAN STOP MESSING UP MY HOUSE.
DO EITHER OF YOUR GRANDSONS OWN A PAIR OF NIKE SOCKS?
SOCKS WITH A BIG BLACK CHECK-MARK ON THEM?
WHY WOULD I PAY EXTRA FOR CHECKMARKS ON HIS SOCKS?
WE'LL BE BACK, I'M SURE.
NICE SHINER, BY THE WAY.

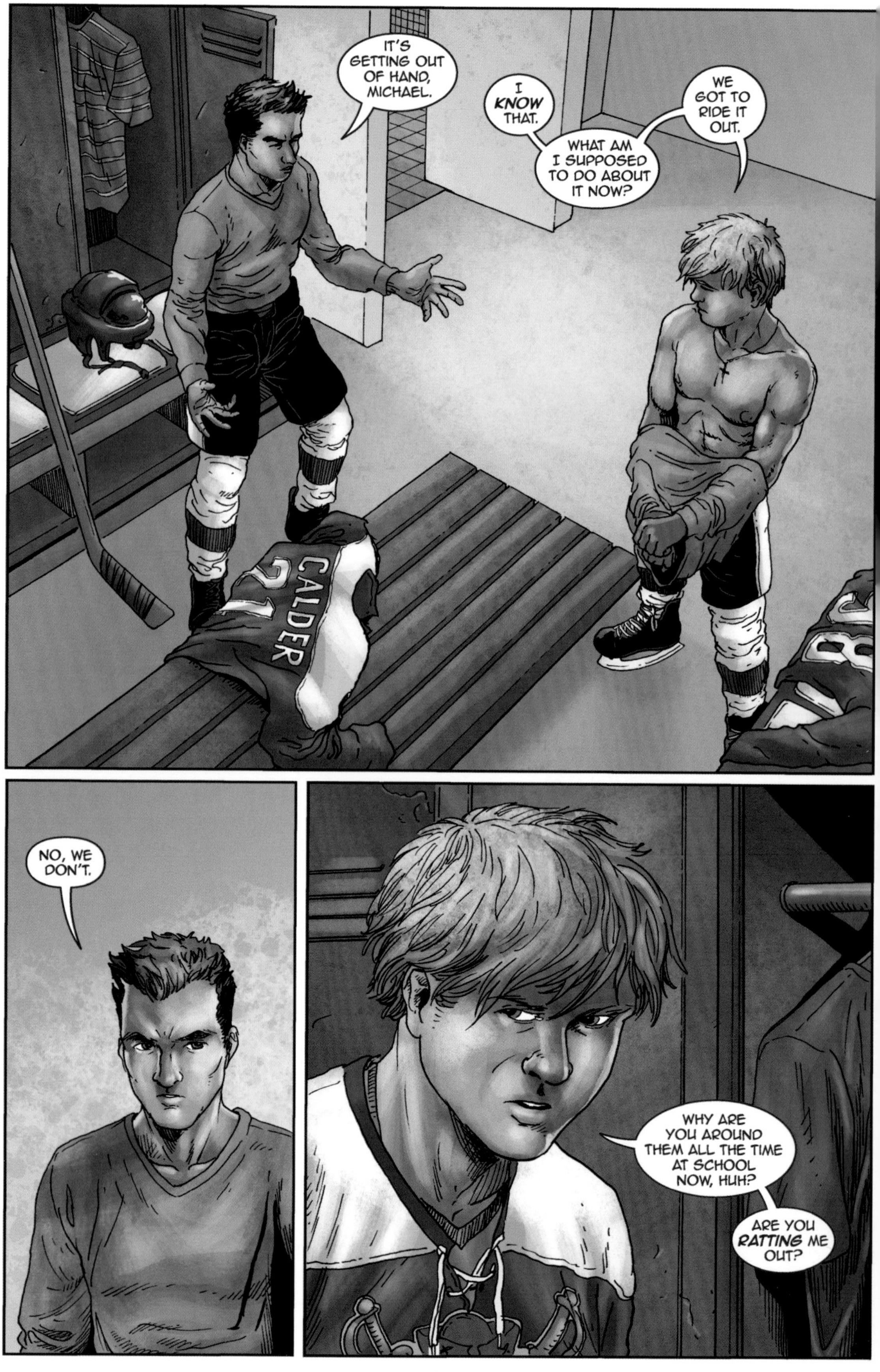
IT'S GETTING OUT OF HAND, MICHAEL.
I KNOW THAT.
WHAT AM I SUPPOSED TO DO ABOUT IT NOW?
WE GOT TO RIDE IT OUT.
CALDER 21
NO, WE DON'T.
WHY ARE YOU AROUND THEM ALL THE TIME AT SCHOOL NOW, HUH?
ARE YOU RATTING ME OUT?

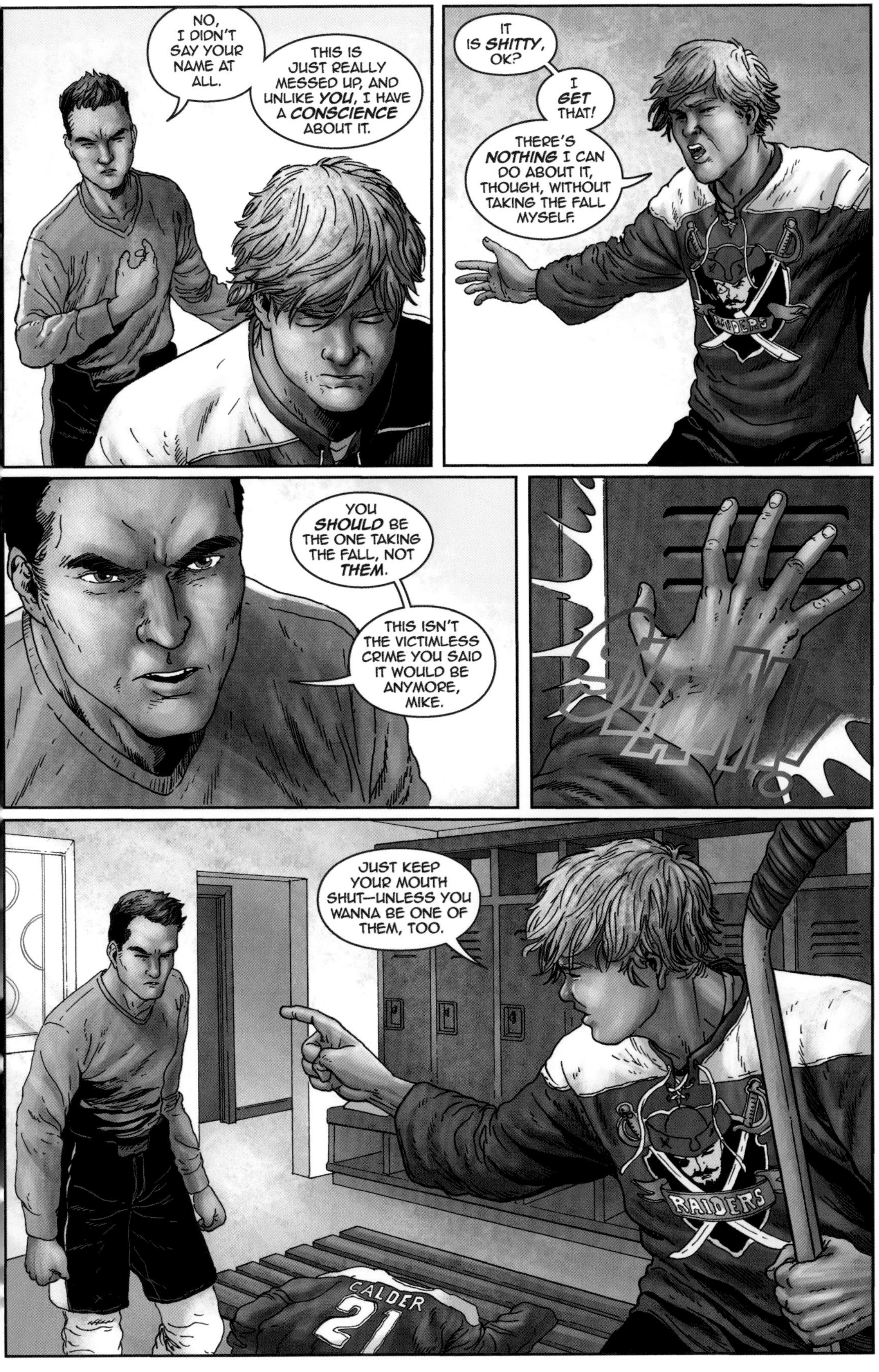
NO, I DIDN'T SAY YOUR NAME AT ALL.
THIS IS JUST REALLY MESSED UP, AND UNLIKE YOU, I HAVE A CONSCIENCE ABOUT IT.
IT IS SHITTY, OK?
I GET THAT!
THERE'S NOTHING I CAN DO ABOUT IT, THOUGH, WITHOUT TAKING THE FALL MYSELF.
RAIDERS
YOU SHOULD BE THE ONE TAKING THE FALL, NOT THEM.
THIS ISN'T THE VICTIMLESS CRIME YOU SAID IT WOULD BE ANYMORE, MIKE.
JUST KEEP YOUR MOUTH SHUT—UNLESS YOU WANNA BE ONE OF THEM, TOO.
RAIDERS
CALDER
21

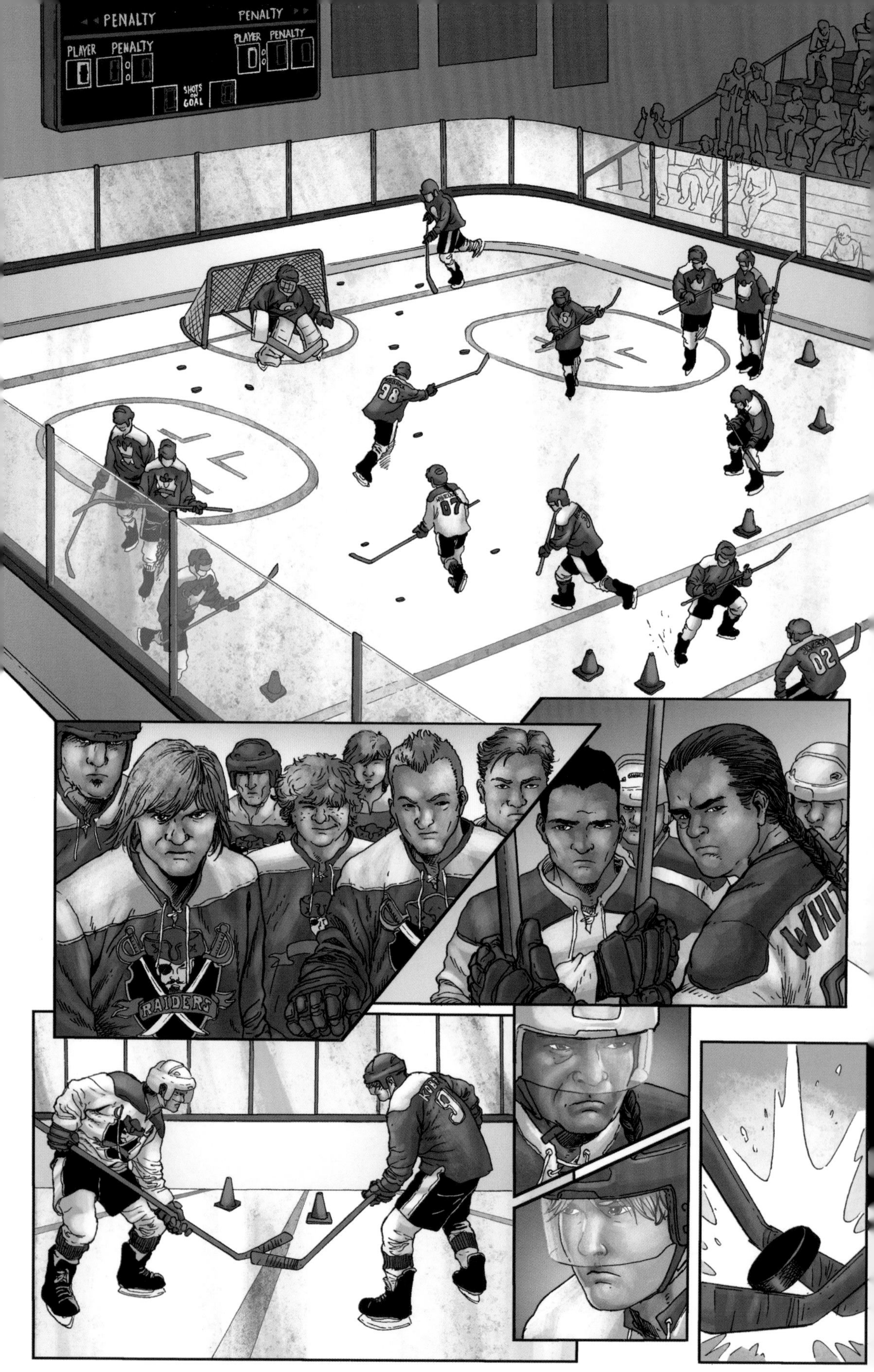
PENALTY
PENALTY
PLAYER PENALTY
PLAYER PENALTY
SHOTS ON GOAL
98
07
02
RAIDERS
WHIT

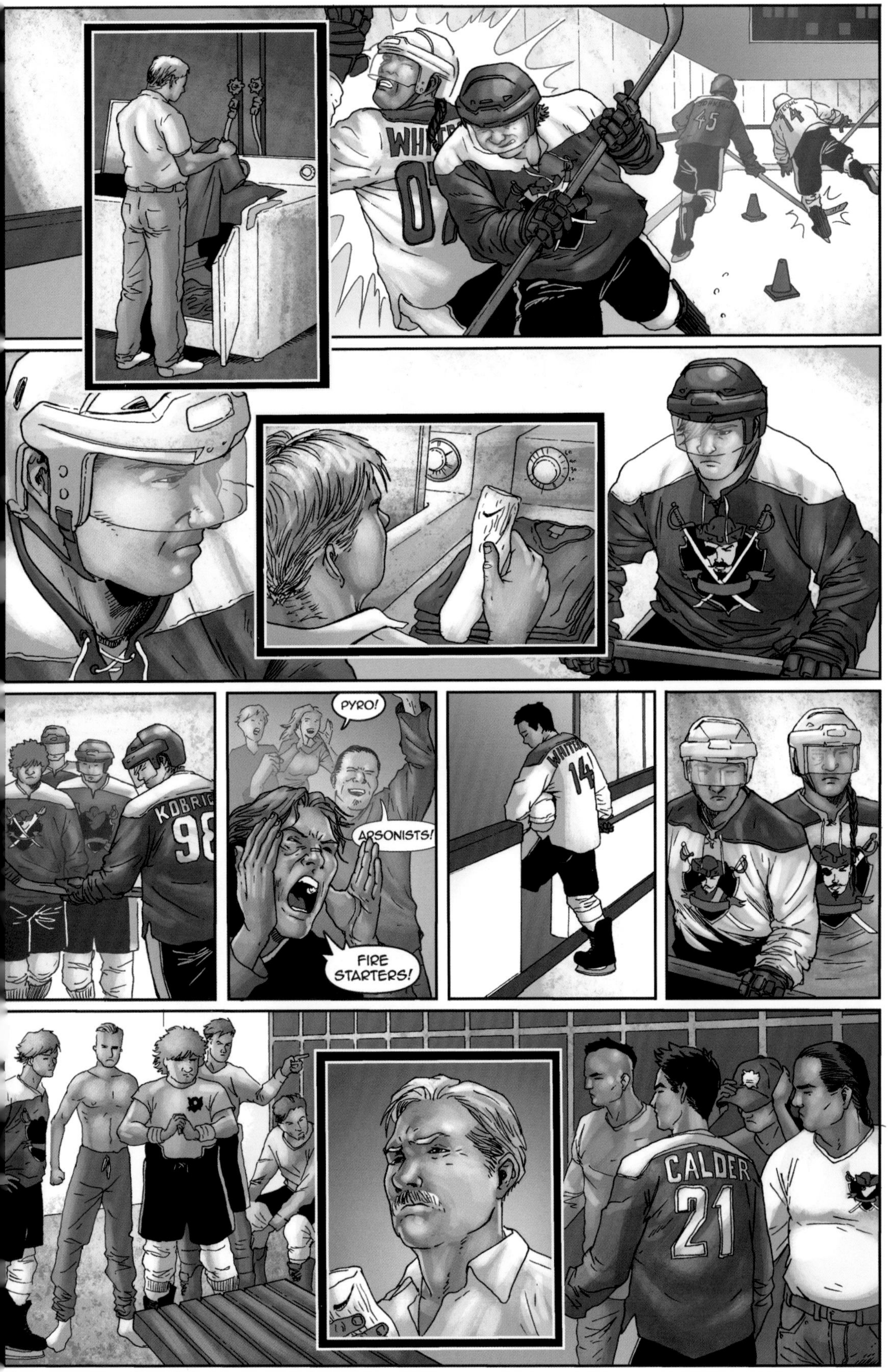

PYRO!
ARSONISTS!
FIRE STARTERS!

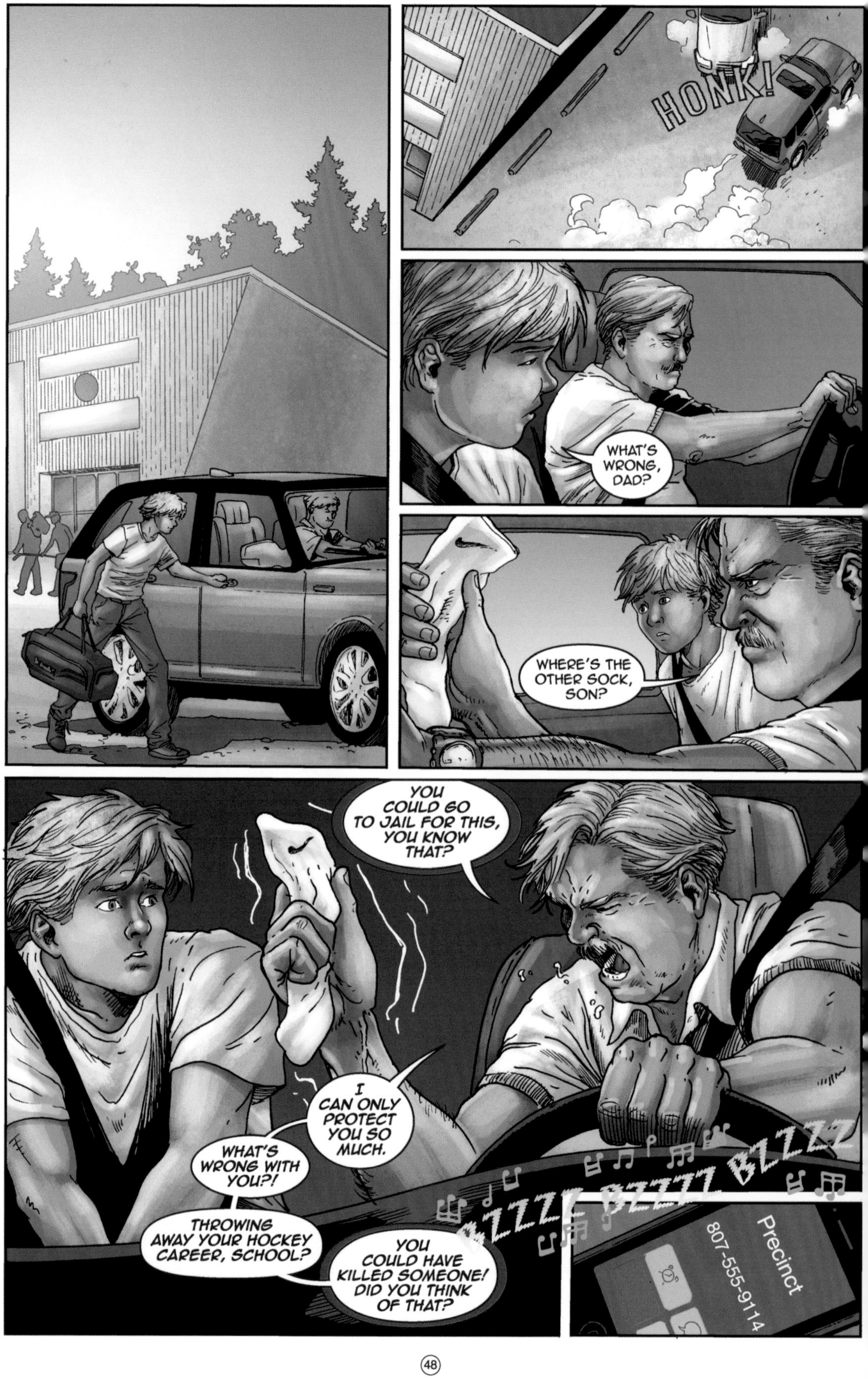
HONK!
WHAT'S WRONG, DAD?
WHERE'S THE OTHER SOCK, SON?
YOU COULD GO TO JAIL FOR THIS, YOU KNOW THAT?
I CAN ONLY PROTECT YOU SO MUCH.
WHAT'S WRONG WITH YOU?!
THROWING AWAY YOUR HOCKEY CAREER, SCHOOL?
YOU COULD HAVE KILLED SOMEONE! DID YOU THINK OF THAT?
BZZZZ BZZZZ BZZZZ
Precinct
807-555-9114

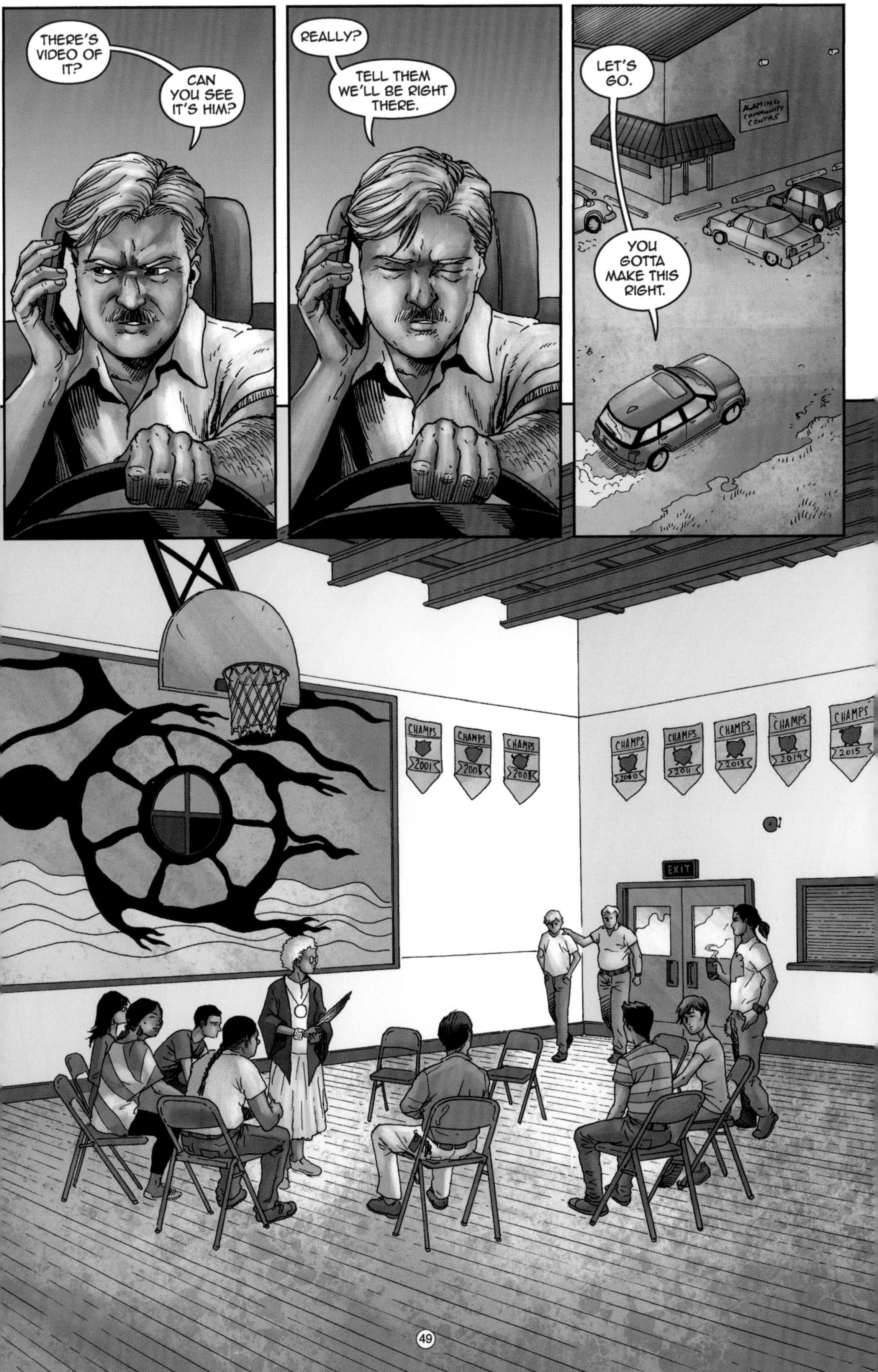

THERE'S VIDEO OF IT?
CAN YOU SEE IT'S HIM?
REALLY?
TELL THEM WE'LL BE RIGHT THERE.
LET'S GO.
COMMUNITY CENTRE
YOU GOTTA MAKE THIS RIGHT.
CHAMPS 2001
CHAMPS
CHAMPS
CHAMPS
CHAMPS 2011
CHAMPS 2013
CHAMPS 2014
CHAMPS 2015
EXIT

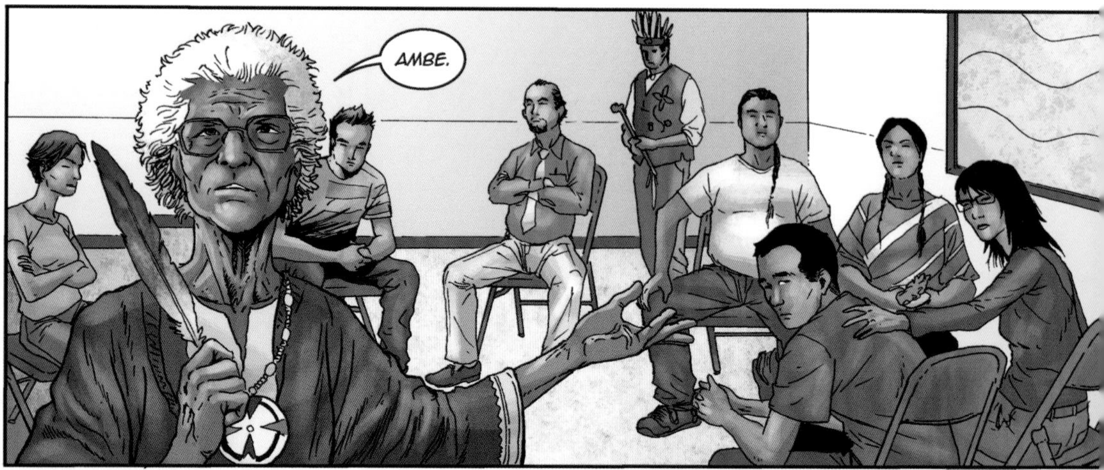
AMBE.

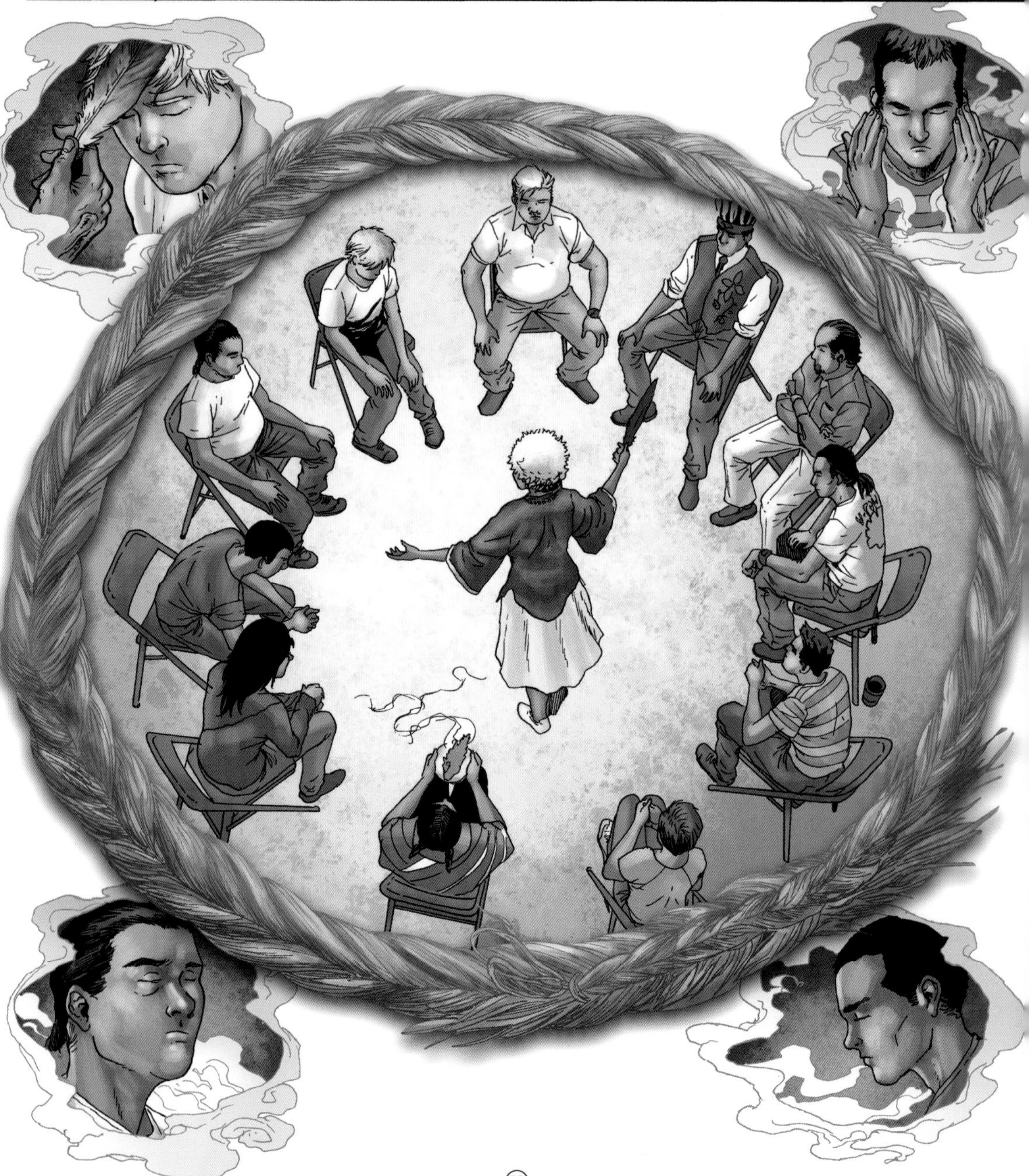

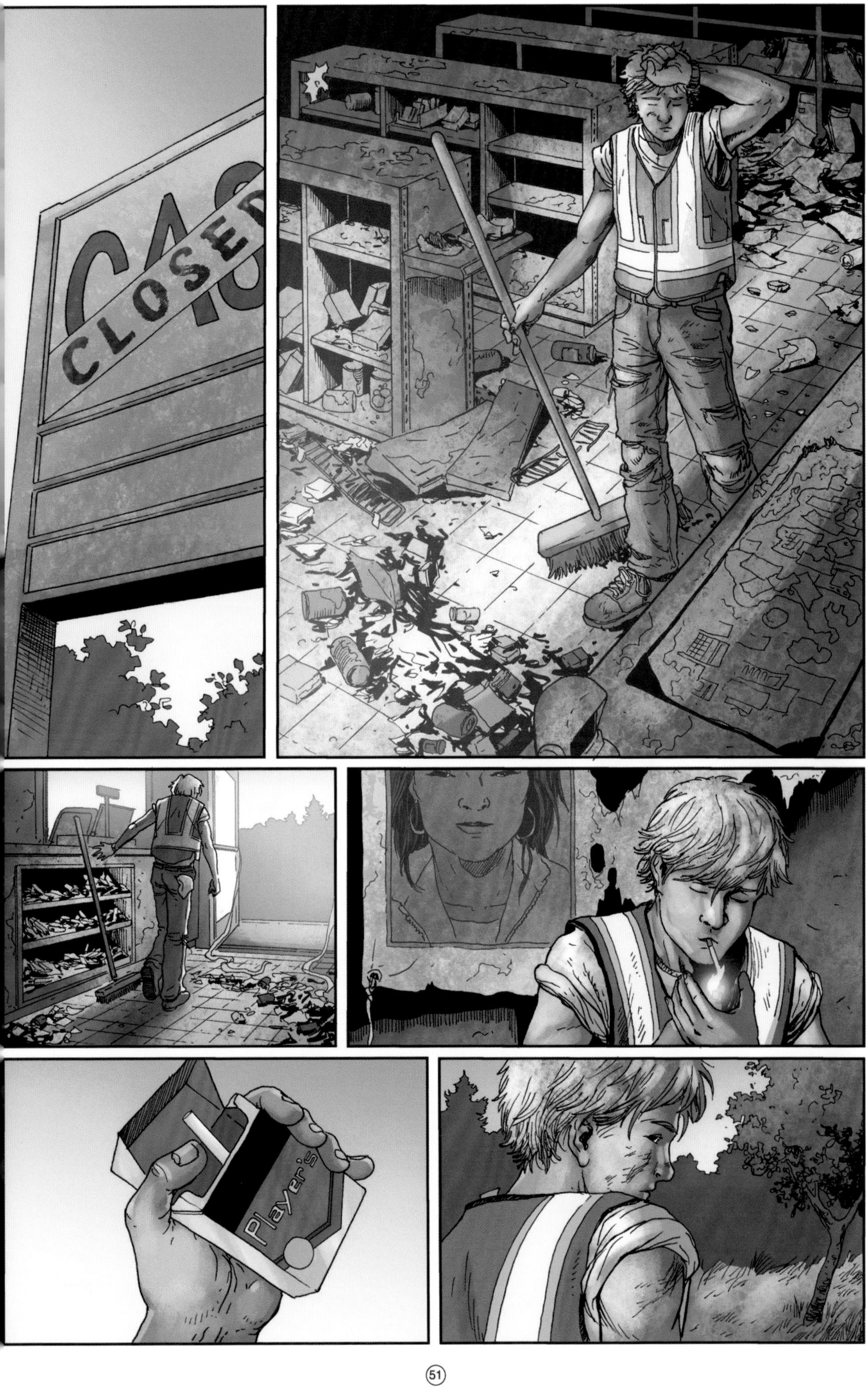
CLOSED
Player's

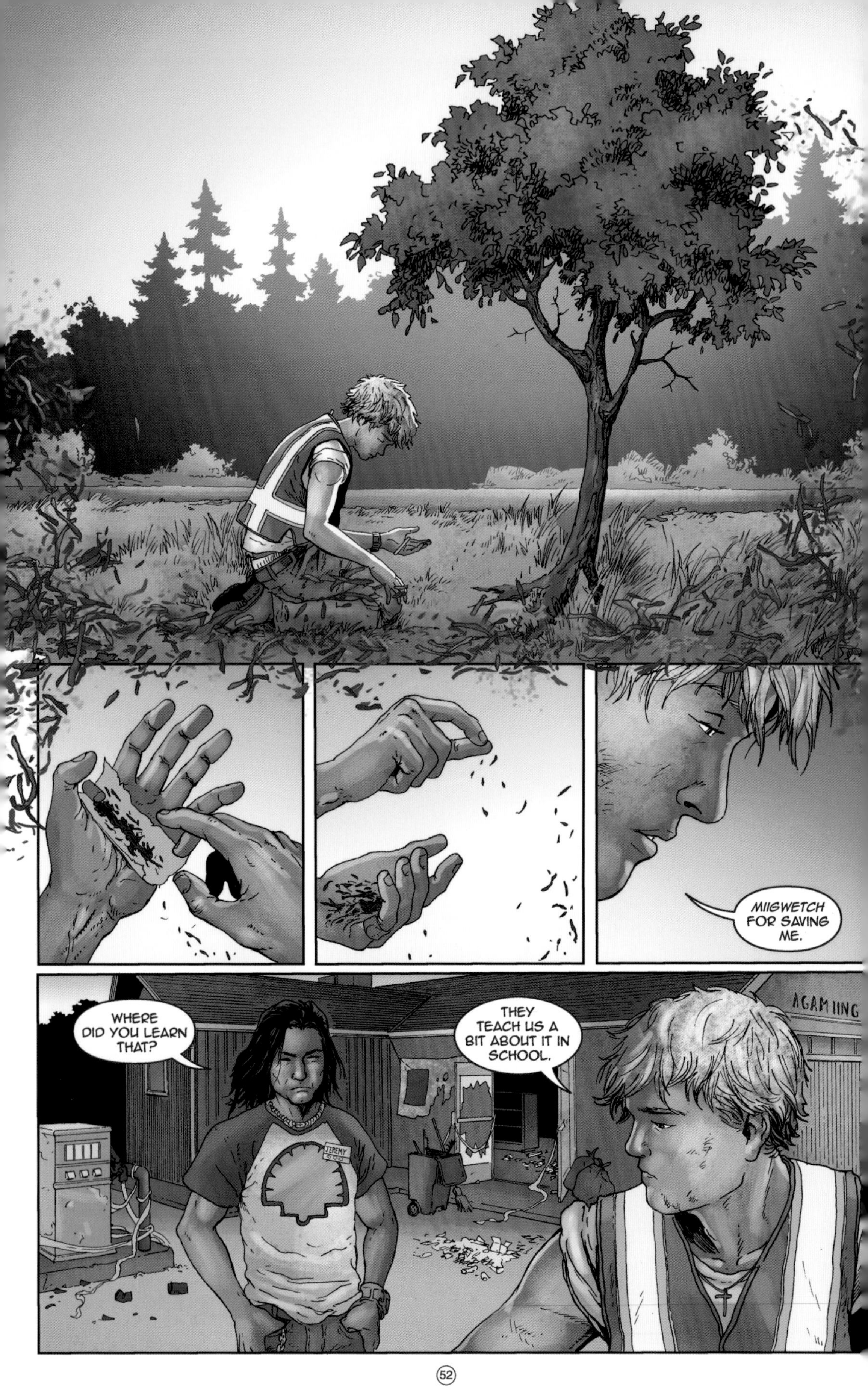
MIIGWETCH FOR SAVING ME.
AGAMIING
WHERE DID YOU LEARN THAT?
THEY TEACH US A BIT ABOUT IT IN SCHOOL.
JEREMY

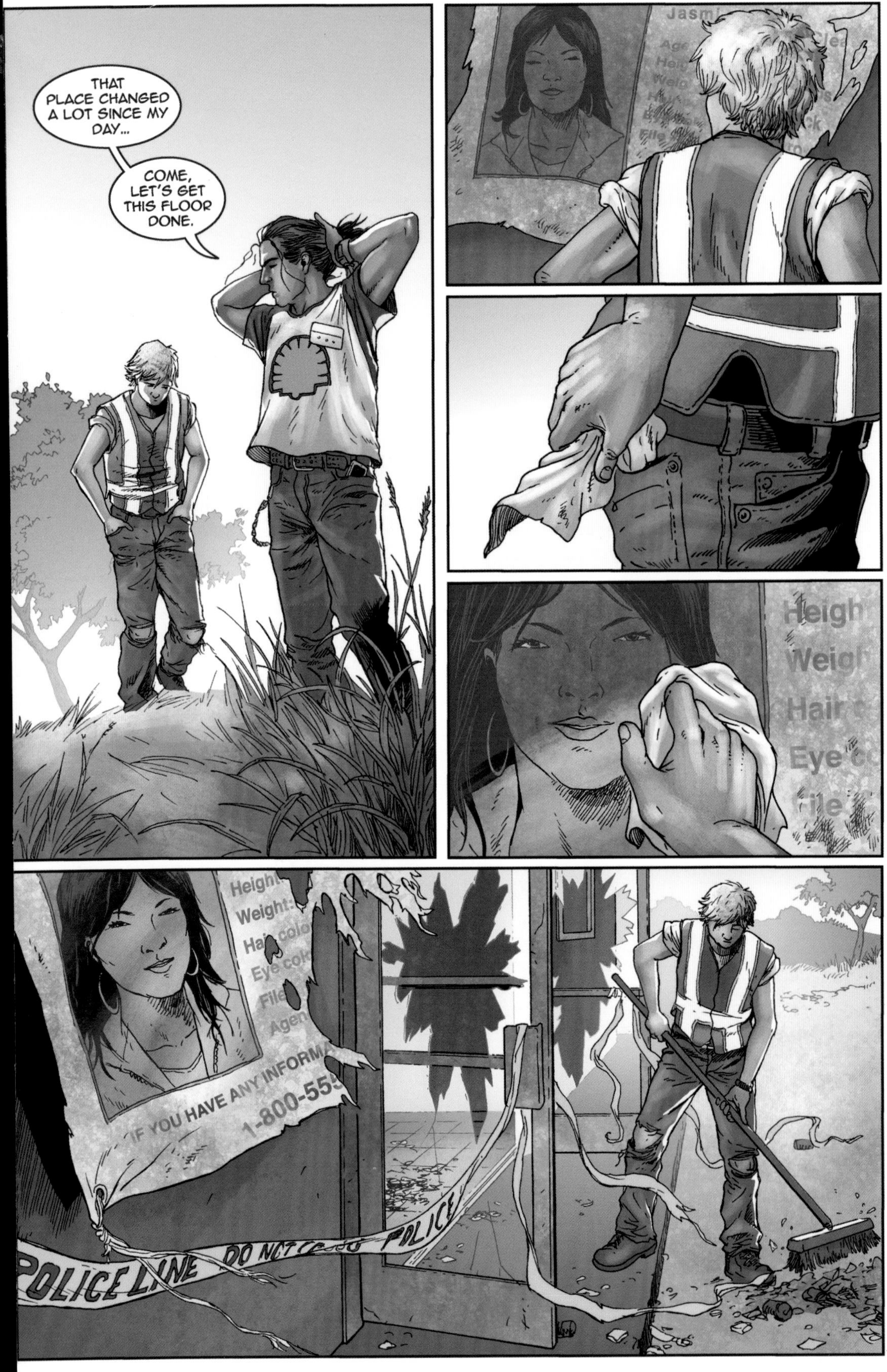
THAT PLACE CHANGED A LOT SINCE MY DAY...
COME, LET'S GET THIS FLOOR DONE.
Height
Weight:
IF YOU HAVE ANY INFORM
1-800-555
POLICE LINE
POLICE

ACKNOWLEDGMENTS

Completing Fire Starters was not easy and I had many who helped me along the way.

First, I would like to thank my father Kirk, my mother Kali, and my stepdad Darren. Without your help and cheerleading, I wouldn't have been a writer to begin with, and without your grand-parenting, I wouldn't have ever found the time to write this story.

Next, I want to thank my family in Couchiching First Nation and Fort Frances, Ontario whose influence resonates in every step I take in this life. I love you all so much.

I want to thank Scott Henderson for giving life to the images in my head. Your vibrant scenes and attention to detail made my story so much stronger and more than I ever thought it could be. I will never be able to thank you enough for your time and dedication to make Fire Starters what it is.

My publishers Annalee Greenberg and Catherine Gerbasi believed in me and encouraged – demanded! – I do this book. Your commitment to Indigenous literature and making me a part of The Debwe Series is overwhelming and I am so honoured to have this book appear among so many great authors. A big thanks, too, to Kirsten and Laina for encouraging me to promote the book nationally – something out of my comfort zone!

Special shout-outs have to go to Barb, Jenni, Desiree, Katie, and Sarah – all of whom make me laugh and love, and support me.

I don't know how to thank my partner Niigaan except to say, you are the best. You work too much but I love you anyways. K'zaagin.

For all Anishinaabe and especially the young ones – keep moving, growing, and living. You inspire me.